BLOOD & BONE

AN ANTHOLOGY OF BODY HORROR BY WOMEN & NON-BINARY WRITERS

Edited by A.R. Ward

With a Foreword by Alex Woodroe

Blood & Bone

An Anthology of Body Horror by Women & Non-Binary Writers

A Ghost Orchid Press Anthology

First published in Great Britain 2021 by Ghost Orchid Press

ISBN (paperback): 978-1-8383915-8-4

ISBN (e-book): 978-1-8383915-9-1

Cover design and book formatting by Claire Saag

I am afraid to own a Body –
I am afraid to own a Soul –
Profound – precarious Property –
Possession, not optional –

Double Estate – entailed at pleasure
Upon an unsuspecting Heir –
Duke in a moment of Deathlessness
And God, for a Frontier.

–*Emily Dickinson,*
"I am afraid to own a Body"

CONTENTS

EDITOR'S NOTE

Readers should be aware that the stories in this volume deal with a range of difficult, potentially triggering subjects including rape and assault, eating disorders, self-harm, mental illness, pregnancy loss and more. Concerned readers may check our list of content warnings at the back of the book for notes on the content of specific stories.

FOREWORD

Our bodies are terrifying.

—Alex Woodroe

One of the greatest things about body horror is that it's unlikely anyone reading this anthology right now is doing so by accident.

You know what you want. You're here because at some point in your life, you've marvelled at and been horrified by the human body. You've looked at your own with suspicious eyes, wondering when it's finally, inevitably, going to betray you. You've poked it and pulled it, questioned it and been questioned by it, and found that neither modern science nor philosophy can give you any answers.

It's been that way since Mary Shelley asked, "if we were to create a new body out of disparate human parts, what would inhabit it?" and used that question to fuel the burning human desire for purpose, identity, and belonging. It wasn't because back in 1818 she wanted *Frankenstein; or, The Modern Prometheus* to break new grounds in the genre of body horror, but because she acknowledged an eternal truth: bodies are horrible. The unknown inside us is equal in terrors to any other unknown in the universe.

The name only came later. A wave of cinema that rippled through the '80s, '90s, and beyond drew loads of attention to the gruesome and depraved, to the ways our bodies changed and lost control, to the ways in which they behaved almost like separate entities to our minds. We basked in the gory glory of films like *Videodrome* and *Cabin Fever*, and established the shape of Body Horror for the next generation. Pushing the boundaries of both gore and imagination ever-further, vivid and cinematic, fearless and metaphorical, it seemed like it could be pushed no further.

Until this moment. Today, right now, we're on a vertex we're fortunate to see first-hand. The collision between brave new independent presses, and authors who have had too little room in Horror for far too long, has created a blast zone of new ideas with more depth than even Shelley could have hoped for. Far beyond just stomach-turning terror, modern Body Horror lives on the edge of where our anatomy meets technology, identity, and good old existential dread. It feeds off the uncertainties in our climates and politics; it draws inspiration from our helpless rage at the changing world around us, and it brings it all together in stories that, ultimately, are nothing short of personal essays about our relationships with our physical selves.

But, like most magic, you have to be open to being amazed. In horror, you have to open up to being horrified. The responsibility for finding meaning and understanding lies on you, the reader. If, while gnashing your teeth through some terrifying tale, you become even a fraction more intimate with what it means to inhabit your body, then the effort will have paid off.

Besides, it's better if we conquer them before they conquer us.

—Alex Woodroe

ALEX WOODROW is the editor of In Somnio *at Tenebrous Press, and is currently working on upcoming projects with CatStone Books and Brigid's Gate Press.*

SIPHONOPHORE

Saoirse Ní Chiaragáin

Who were we before we were his? Who were the women we once were? We can trace the stitches, carefully, with two disparate hands. When we touch, palm-to-palm, are we sisters or are we lovers? If nothing else, we are not one. We can feel one another, pulled together as tightly as corset laces, stranger meeting stranger's flesh. One body that feels like a crowded room. A community of loves, losses, and lives, stitched crudely together in service of a monster. To make for him a bride.

The doctor is not a religious man. How could he be, when he has seen fit to insult God not once, but twice? Still, we notice with an uneasy irony, he has fallen into the same traps as that great creator. We feel every bit akin to that carved rib. Mutilated and manipulated into a mate for what came before us—his real masterpiece. Parts of us still remember the Bible well, and hope to bring knowledge into our rotting brain, to force revolt into its greying folds. To be the Eve he created us to be.

Other parts of us remember a different story. We remember Lilith, rejected bride of Adam, mother of demons. In our darker moments, we hope to unleash demons of our own. Tear the laboratory asunder, let the doctor and his creature burn. Let us burn, too. Anything to return to the peace of the grave.

Does he feel the same, our bridegroom? Does he feel the attraction and repulsion of his many parts, the multitudes he contains? Does he dream our same dark dreams?

Some of us hesitate to consider him an ally. Is he a lover or a brother? While, yes, he was also robbed from the slumber of his tombs, and forged into a festering fraternity of spent skin, we are not the same. The doctor surged life into him, creating a monster in his own image. We, on the other hand, were created to satisfy the monster. To be his prey, his partner.

Not content with breathing life into the dead, Dr Frankenstein wishes to create life anew. Or rather, he wants us to be the conduit through which new life is made. Our flesh collectively ripples into goosebumps with the approach of nightfall. A uniform response, each of us dreading the inevitable. The doctor eases us down on the cold flagstones, removing our thin shift. The monster, unblinking and impassive, stands to the side waiting for his own undressing.

The doctor learns early on that scorched earth will not bear fruit. There is not enough spark left within our rotten parts to swell with promise. Some of us were mothers, maternal touch left longing and bereft, never to cradle our babies again. Some of us were yet babies ourselves, still soft and ripening when our short lives ended for the first time. When we hold our hands together, as though in prayer, mothers comfort children.

He experiments with fresher bodies. Girls taken from mortuary slabs, still the whisper of warmth about them. As soon as they breathe their last, he is there to collect what he has been promised. They never join us—never fully. The organ is always rejected. Not fit for his divine purpose. Yet we feel a queer kinship to those girls, already dead like us, bodies cut and sewn thereafter. Wherever they now slumber, we hope they remain undisturbed.

In his absence, while he collects, we wander the lab. We trace the spines of great volumes of knowledge, their contents obscure, the leather bounds as taut and browned as our own skins. The monster lurks. He dares not approach without Frankenstein's instruction. From the shadowy corners of the room, he drinks us in with dead man's eyes, all light drained from them. How must we look to him? When we try to imagine ourselves, we think of rag dolls, the likes of which our mothers and grandmothers fashioned from fraying cloth. We think of patchwork quilts. We think of fields of varying verdant shades, dissected by stone walls, punctuated by stiles.

We note, with a spectrum of sorrow, our differences from these things. Neither beloved nor held in the little hands of a child like a rag doll. Not warm like the quilt. Not free as the fields. All are artifacts of a world apart, a world in which we no longer belong.

When the doctor arrives home, it is in a whirlwind of anger and agitation. He will not rest until the experiment succeeds. Against all rationality, all mercy, he charges on. One night, the sutures in our abdomen freshly sewn, a ghastly look of inspiration settles across his features. He wastes no time. The following morning, he brings a girl.

She is young—old enough to have been wandering alone, but not too old to be easily enticed. We know her first by her careful footsteps, stepping nervously across the threshold. We hear his muffled reassurances leading her across the floor with the deftness and elegance of a waltz. She hesitates as they reach the door of the lab. He coos to her, something we cannot decipher, yet the tender quality to his voice causes us to shudder. It is a voice we have heard on the rare occasions when we refuse to capitulate to his and the monster's desires. A tone of warning, veiled in warmth, which is usually followed by violence.

The door clicks open, hanging wide and heavy on its hinges, and we see her shadow cast down into our murky abode. Thinned and lengthened by the light behind her, we watch as her shadow descends, meeting the dark of the lab and joining it. Her frail form follows, the doctor looming behind. We see her eyes find us in the gloom, how the breath is knocked from her narrow chest by the sight. Before she has a chance to scream, the doctor's blade is pulled smoothly across her throat.

Our own throat cannot produce the sounds we long to make in that moment. We wail, a host of voices crying in unison, as we watch the girl fall to the ground, tresses of her hair mopping her still-spreading blood. We rasp, falling to our knees, hacking great gusts of grief onto the stone floor. We could spend hours there, all of us, mourning this poor thing. But the monster grabs hold of us, ushers us to our feet and away from the body, all on the doctor's command.

We are silent as the doctor rips us open. We do not watch as he places the girl's womb into our dry cavity. We go limp as we are sewn together again and fed to the monster, the doctor eager for his seed to take root in the newly laid fertile land. We do not sleep, even as Frankenstein and the monster sleep. Instead, we lie awake, dead eyes drinking in the darkness, our festering minds plotting, plotting, plotting.

The experiment fails. The girl's organs wither within us, infected by our putrescence. This time, Victor blames the monster. He has overestimated the creature's virility. He paces the lab, convincing himself that the experiment can succeed only by joining living cells—his own, and that of another girl. Had we words to speak, we would tell him how foolish it all sounds. But he is too far gone, his ego swollen beyond the limits of sanity, and he disappears into the twilight to fetch another child.

Though time is scarce, we attempt to relay our intentions to the monster. We approach him, standing in his corner, as silent and foreboding as a suit of armour. Tenderly, we take his hand in ours. We attempt to pull apart the stitches, hoping to touch the raw edges of our skins to his. But our dexterity is poor, foreign fingers struggling to work in tandem. The whole time, he mutely watches, his empty gaze studying our own. At last, a fingernail manages to hook a thread and pry a suture loose, but no sooner do we pull than the door above opens.

Again, our ears prick to the sound of light footfalls, the girlish gait entering more willingly this time. Perhaps he has lured her with treats rather than promises, coaxing her more readily to her demise.

The door to the lab swings open, and her little shadow greets us. We stand with our back to the monster, as though in defence of him, concealing the pulled threads of his hand.

She is smaller than the last, a sparrow of a girl, and she regards us with a sense of childlike wonder, eyes glassy as a doll's. Any fear within her is tempered with curiosity as she takes a tentative step towards us, her tiny hand twitching towards touch. The doctor's shadow falls over her, and his knife is not far behind. There is a pinprick of shock in her eyes, before they drain of light and she slackens.

We do not fall with her this time. We stand, the monster's hand in ours, and watch as the doctor gets to work. The girl hollowed, he leads us to the slab and opens us, feeding the child's flesh into the hungry cavity. Once sewn again, he does not bother to move us from the slab. Instead, he mounts us there, still clothed, and desperately sows the new flesh. I can feel the monster's gaze upon us. Is it jealousy he feels, or despair? Is he our lover or our brother? As the doctor finishes and retreats upstairs, the monster comes to our side. In the dark of the lab, the child's body waiting somewhere in shadow, he takes our hand.

We feel the heat of the doctor's expulsion settle within us with a sickly sensation. We cannot allow the experiment to succeed. We find the scalpel among his tools beside the slab and cut the fresh stitches. Our hands dig into the cold flesh, finding the cooling organs, and place them gently to one side. We will bury them later, alongside the rest of the girl. We will not replace them, however. She deserves a greater dignity than to be buried with the doctor's seed inside her.

The monster approaches, and we cut the stitches on his wrist. His hand removed, we do the same to our own. We touch the open wound against his, and in a moment feel all the lives within him, and he all the lives within us. We quickly find that such a configuration would be inelegant in the long run. To move as one, to meet together and organise, we must find a more suitable shape.

We spend the night—the monster and us—cutting and re-sewing stitches. We forge our own anatomy, finding a body through trial and error that will best serve our needs. Rib to carved rib, pulling closer with each draw of the needle. By morning we are born again, a new whole, a town made flesh, a creature unlike any of God's creations.

We hold greater knowledge now, a wedding gift from our more recent parts. Excerpts from books read to us when we were still just the monster, our fetid brain coaxed to life by the words of our creator. Memories of his voice reading from his scientific tomes, breathing sparks into our tired minds, drawn from the sleep of the abyss. We remember his recitation of a biological study. Of creatures who live in the vast oceans, unable to exist alone, but thriving as a community of parts. Among them, the Portuguese Man O'War, a monstrous thing that stings and can kill those who wander too closely. Creatures of the order siphonophore. Yes, we remember. Yes, we like that.

We move, four legs and four arms, to the girl. We place her gently in the shadows for now. She will be buried when the work is done.

Whether the doctor likes it or not. Four hands are armed with scalpels and saws. Four feet wait, poised to spring forward.

The doctor rises with the dawn. We hear his feet upon the beams above us, our four ears attuned to the sound. The door to the lab opens, welcoming his shadow. He descends most of the steps before he sees us. He hasn't our speed, and we are swiftly upon him. Our bulk, the weight of so many bodies and lives, crashes down upon him. We slice at him with the blades, our two mouths finding his warm flesh and tearing with desperate teeth.

We cannot say how long it lasts, the beautiful destruction of Doctor Victor Frankenstein. When all that remains of him are disparate parts, we undo our stitches again, and welcome him into our fold. Not out of any sense of duty. He is not a father, he is not a lover, and he is not a god. But his flesh holds knowledge we need. Understandings of bodies and the recreation of life. His skin cries out as it meets ours, fading warmth to sepulchre cold. He spits admonishments, calls us an abomination, but his voice is buried beneath ours. He is but one, and we are so many.

Moving six legs before six arms, torsos conjoined into a lithe thorax, we cradle the girl and ascend the stairs. In the cool of night, we shovel dirt with six hands and lay her to rest. We will not be able to stay long. The missing girls will be traced soon enough, and villagers will come for Victor's pound of flesh. We must seek refuge elsewhere. But for now, we lay ourselves upon the grass beside the mound of earth. Above us, with our six eyes cast skywards, we can see every star.

SAOIRSE NÍ CHIARAGÁIN is an Irish writer living in Berlin, Germany. Her work has appeared in Novel Noctule, and will appear in the upcoming anthology 99 Tiny Terrors *edited by Jennifer Brozek. Her co-written feature film,* Consentuality*, is currently in development with Screen Ireland. You can follow her at @MiseryVulture on Twitter.*

THICKER THAN WATER

Kristin Cleaveland

Allie's mama had the blood rain and everybody knew it. People said it had been in the family since way back when—Allie's great-great-grandma had it, and when they held her funeral service the ceiling dripped blood over the whole church. After that everyone in Allie's family had their services in the graveyard, because the church ladies had to scrub for hours to get all the blood stains to come up.

No one knew where the blood rain came from. Some said Allie's great-great grandma was a witch; others said someone must have cursed the family. But even the oldest people in town didn't know for sure. The blood never fell from the sky, it only rained inside. People said maybe the ladies with the blood rain just had too much trapped in their heads, like glass jars filled past the threads and all the way to the brim. But everyone got used to it, and some had started to think it died out until it showed up strong in Allie's mama.

When Allie's mama was born there was no more blood than normal, but soon the house began to drizzle blood when she cried, and Allie's grandma had to hush her up or she'd have a mess on her hands. The neighbours gave her some of their old sheets to drape over her furniture, and she learned fast to cover the pots on the stove so the food wouldn't taste of iron.

The family got along all right, even if Allie's mama had to sit outside the schoolhouse and listen through the window. At home she sat on the back porch when it was warm, and in the winter she carried a rag to wipe the walls and corners when they started to drip. She didn't sew or cook much, due to the mess, but she grew up so pretty that eventually the boy who would be Allie's daddy said he guessed he wouldn't mind a little blood on his shirts.

They got married in the churchyard on a bright sunny day, and Allie's mama put her white dress on behind the church while her aunties held up sheets around her. She carried white daisies and everyone agreed she was the prettiest bride they'd ever seen. Allie's daddy wore a bright red rose on his lapel and didn't stop smiling once the whole day.

Before too long, baby Allie came along and everyone waited to see if she had the blood rain too. But when she cried it was just like normal, and everyone sighed and was happy and Allie's daddy passed around whiskey to celebrate. Allie's mama said it was a good thing too because there were enough stains in the house already, but she looked just a little sad when she said it.

Allie's mama loved her baby girl, but more and more blood started showing. She had to cover the bassinet with old sheets and towels, or the dripping from the ceiling would wake the baby. Sometimes Allie woke anyway and watched the red spots bloom on the sheets like petals on a flower. Still, she didn't cry much. People said she must know her mama cried enough for both of them.

When Allie learned to walk, her mama never put socks on her feet because they'd stain as soon as she set her down. Sheets and towels piled up in the washtub. Allie's daddy rarely raised his voice, but one time he yelled that he was tired of eating biscuits with salty red butter. Allie's mama didn't cry, but the whole house dripped all night, even when Allie's daddy said he was sorry and it wasn't her fault.

Then one day Allie's grandma passed away real sudden. Allie's mama cried for three days straight, and she was so sick with the blood rain that people wondered if she'd even show up to the service in the graveyard. But finally her aunties coaxed her out and filled up a tub behind the sheets on the clothesline, and helped her scrub herself and put on her black dress that didn't show the spots.

Little Allie held her mama's hand and never made a sound as they lowered her grandma into the ground. Allie's mama cried like her heart was breaking and couldn't even sing the hymns, which some people said was unchristian because her mama was in heaven and it wasn't the end of the world. Allie's daddy patted her mama's shoulder and looked solemn in his best shirt with only a few red dots here and there.

It got harder to keep up with the blood rain after that. Allie learned to follow her mama around with a rag, and sometimes she stood on a chair with the mop to reach the corners up by the ceiling. Allie's mama hugged her, and read her stories, and sang songs that her own mama sang to her. But still she was always sad, and Allie's books all had red fingerprints in the corners.

One day Allie's daddy smiled and told her that her mama was going to be happy again real soon, because there was a new baby on the way. Allie looked at her mama and she nodded yes, it was true, but her smile looked so tired. Allie wondered how her mama would keep up with the washing now that there would be diapers and rags every day. She gave her mama a hug and smelled the sharp tang of her hair. "I love you, baby," Allie's mama whispered, and her voice sounded like it did when she talked about Allie's grandma. Then she said, "I'm sorry," and Allie didn't know why. She kept saying it, softer and softer, and Allie hugged her mama and patted her hair until her hand was red and sticky.

Allie's mama spent a lot of time in her room lying down, because the baby made her tired and sometimes she got sick in a bucket. Allie's daddy said she'd feel better soon, and he made Allie pancakes and told her jokes, but quiet, in case Allie's mama was sleeping. One day Allie was eating her supper when a big red drop splattered right in the middle of her plate. She looked up and saw a red spot on the ceiling, and then she heard a howl from upstairs that sounded half animal and all sorrow. Allie's daddy dropped his napkin and ran, and the wailing got louder and she heard her daddy curse out loud and suddenly the blood was everywhere, it was in the food and in the sink and in the washtub and Allie looked up and watched it fall until her eyes stung and her whole face was red.

When her daddy brought Allie to her aunties, they sat her in a tub and took hard soap and scrubbed until both her skin and the water in the tub were bright red. They wrapped her in the whitest towel she had ever seen and gave her something hot to drink that made her feel sleepy. She heard her aunties whispering and understood enough to know that the baby had come too early and the doctor had come too late. Somehow Allie knew she'd never go back to the house where she'd been born. She stared up at the smooth white ceiling until she couldn't hold her eyes open anymore.

A few days later, Allie held her daddy's hand in the churchyard. He wore a black suit and Allie wore a white dress, because she didn't have a black one and people said it didn't matter anyway, she was only little. Allie's aunties sang the hymns, but she didn't know the words. She just stared at the white flowers on her mama's dark coffin, thinking it didn't seem right only black and white. She didn't notice right away when the red petals bloomed on her white dress and speckled her white tights. She kept on looking at the flowers that were white, then pink, then crimson red, until all the ladies were clutching their red hymnals and black Bibles and screaming, running for the church as the sky opened up and cried for Allie and her mama.

KRISTIN CLEAVELAND writes horror and dark fiction. Her work has been published by Ghost Orchid Press, Quill and Crow Publishing House, Black Telephone Magazine, *and more. Find her on Twitter as @KristinCleaves.*

GASTRIC

Caitlin Marceau

The room smells like rubbing alcohol and floor cleaner, and although it's warm, Billie is cold in her thin hospital gown. She shivers on the gurney, partly because of the thin fabric that opens in the back, partly because of nerves. Her husband sits on the worn-in armchair next to the bed and scrolls through his Instagram feed, stopping every few minutes to like a photo. She pretends not to notice when he double taps an image of a twenty-something woman in a bikini.

"What time is it?" she asks, fidgeting with the plastic identification bracelet fastened around her wrist. There are no clocks on the walls, which only heightens her suspicion that time isn't passing at all within the confines of her room. Alfie swipes his finger across his phone and frowns.

"It's just after two. The doctor's late."

"Maybe this is a sign," she says, immediately regretting her decision to speak up about the issue.

Alfie sighs, leaning to one side so he can slip his phone into his pocket, before locking eyes with her. "Are we really having this conversation again?"

"No, I'm not trying to… well, yeah, actually," she finally admits, looking away from him. "I'm nervous and, honestly, I still really don't know if I want to do this. It just, I don't know, it seems extreme."

"Billie, how many times have you tried to lose weight on your own?"

"I don't know."

"Neither do I, but I know it's been a lot. And I know this because I've had to live with you through each weird diet phase you've gone through. There were shakes, bars, something involving wheatgrass and a juicer, fasting, group meetings, pre-made meals—"

"I know, I know. But diet culture is fucked and science shows that diets don't work and—"

"They don't work for *you.*" The words are like a slap in the face and she feels winded. "But that's okay," he continues in a softer voice, "having that level of willpower is tough and just isn't for everyone. And like, even having the willpower to lose the weight without help doesn't mean you'll have the willpower to keep it off. It just doesn't seem like something you'd be able to do. But the procedure you're going to have? It'll be *super* manageable for you afterwards. That way, you won't have the fear of getting, uh, you know, *fat* again looming over you for the rest of your life."

She looks down at herself and runs a hand over her stomach, gently feeling her body through the threadbare gown. It's soft and Rubenesque and—despite what her husband thinks—beautiful. She'd always been bigger than the other girls growing up, a fact that had never bothered her until her grandma had said something about it in front of her family over turkey dinner one Christmas. It had been the start of a lifelong battle with weight, self-love, and her ability to navigate the world comfortably. She'd continued to gain weight through most of high school, but lost a fair amount after puberty hit her like a brick a year before graduation. It had been this leaner body that she'd started college with, and the one Alfie had fallen in love with nearly ten years ago.

She'd started gaining weight before their wedding when the stress of planning the event had felt like too much. It hadn't been enough to bother her, but Alfie had started to notice and comment on the change. He began acting cold towards her, less physically affectionate, and it wasn't long after that that his eyes began wandering when they were out in public. She didn't want to call it quits with him—she *loved* him—so she decided the only reasonable thing to do was wage war on her body. Unfortunately, it was an uphill battle that left her heavier than when she'd started. While she wasn't angry with the change in her body, it was getting harder to ignore the judgmental comments and sideways glances her husband had been giving her. When he brought up the procedure, she felt like the only way to save her marriage was to agree to it.

But sitting on the uncomfortable bed in the sterile room, Billie was regretting her decision.

"You keep saying 'fat' like it's a bad word. It's not. And it hurts when you talk like this," she admits.

He rolls his eyes in annoyance and crosses his arms over his chest. "I'm sorry if I hurt your feelings, but let's be honest about this. This operation is your best shot at a *normal* life." He stresses the word. "Don't you want that? Don't you want to be able to shop at any store you want? Don't you want to be able to run after our kids, you know, when we have them?"

She opens her mouth to argue her point, but the doctor chooses this moment to show up. He's a tall man with brown locks and a receding hairline. He's dressed in navy scrubs and a white lab coat, and he carries a silver clipboard that comically dwarfs the papers resting atop it. He pulls a pen from his breast pocket and clicks the end of it before scribbling something at the top of a page.

"Today's the big day!" he says with a smile, looking up from the sheet of paper. "How are you feeling?"

"Excited," Alfie answers for her. "We're both very excited."

"Good! I'm glad to hear! So I'm just going to—"

"Actually," Billie interrupts, "I'm pretty nervous about everything. And I know this is last minute, but I'm just… I'm having second thoughts about everything, you know?" she admits, despite her husband's audible annoyance.

"That's perfectly normal," he says, crossing the room and taking a seat at the end of her gurney. "What's on your mind?"

"I'm worried I'm making a mistake with this. That I'm having something so invasive done to lose a few pounds and that—"

"It's invasive, yes, but minimally so! Remember, everything is being done laparoscopically, so while you'll have a few scars afterwards, each will be quite small—the biggest one will be where we insert the device and it won't even be two inches—and they should mostly fade away over time. As for your comment about it being a few pounds, remember that we're hoping this operation will get you down by almost a hundred pounds and that weight loss is nearly impossible for people with your BMI. And while this procedure isn't a quick fix, it's a tool that can help you drop the excess weight."

"Yeah, I guess."

"If it's any reassurance, I know that if my daughters were fat they'd be happier thin and I'd have them do this same surgery in a heartbeat," he says happily. "Besides, just think of how good it'll feel to be pretty, right?"

"That's what I keep telling her," Alfie adds.

The comments sting and upset her. She hates their conflation of beauty and weight, and how they've weaponized her size to cut at her sense of self-worth. Her face turns crimson and shame sets in, embarrassed at her husband's quick agreement with the doctor. *Am I not already pretty?* she asks him with her eyes. *Do you find me repulsive?*

Looking at the hospital band on her wrist and the unfriendly room, she already knows the answer.

"So," the doctor continues, not giving Billie a chance to speak, "I'm just going to go over what we're going to be doing today, answer any last-minute questions you might have, and then you'll be directed to the first floor for some pre-op blood work. Sounds good?"

"Yes."

"Excellent! So, today we're going to be inserting the Gastra-Sphaera GR into your stomach laparoscopically. Pre-insertion, the device is a little smaller than a loonie, but once we inflate it with the slow release hormone solution, it'll have a diameter of roughly two and a half—maybe three—inches. It'll be fixed to the wall of your stomach, so there's no risk of you accidentally passing it."

"Okay. Will I feel it? Like, after the operation, when I wake up, will I feel it inside?"

"You might initially. Some patients say it feels like a small weight has been placed in their stomachs, others don't notice it at all. Less than 0.03% of patients report feeling the device after the three-month adjustment period. So if you do feel it, it'll only be a temporary discomfort, especially since the solution in the device is released gradually over the next eighteen months."

"Okay."

"You'll be placed under general anaesthesia for the procedure and kept under observation overnight, just to be safe. Assuming all goes well, you'll be back home this time tomorrow. Now, I just want to reiterate that this isn't a cure for obesity," she shifts uncomfortably at the use of the harsh clinical term, "but a tool to get it under control. Because of the weight and size of the Gastra-Sphaera GR, you're going to feel full faster, and thanks to the slow-release hormone to help control your body's production of Ghrelin you're not going to be hungry or have many food cravings. This will give you roughly eighteen months to re-learn nutrition, how to eat a balanced diet, and how to practise better portion control. If you stick to the plan we've given you and put in the work, you'll be able to successfully lose the hundred pounds and keep it off. Exciting, right?"

"Very," Alfie answers.

Billie just nods her head.

"Did you have any questions for me before I get going?" Dr Fortin asks happily.

She does, dozens of them, but shakes her head and smiles.

"Great! Let's get you downstairs for the blood work and get this show on the road!"

With that, he leads her out of the room and down the hall. Alfie watches her go before turning his attention back to his phone.

"Your name?"

"Billie Ouellet."

"And you have an appointment today?"

"Yes, with Dr Fortin. It's for the two-week follow-up and to have the sutures removed."

"I'll need your Medicare."

Billie opens her wallet and takes out the card, passing it to the woman. The receptionist looks at the card before she places it in the designated groove of the manual card imprinter, places a sheet of prescription paper on top, and slides the handle of the machine. Billie raises an eyebrow at the old device, surprised that the hospital is still using Knuckle-Busters given all their modern technology. The receptionist does this two more times—one on a second sheet of prescription paper and the other on a hospital form—before handing back the card and motioning to the nearby waiting area.

Billie takes a seat, shoving the card back into her wallet, and looks around the familiar space. The walls are eggshell white and decorated with abstract art in sky blue and grass green, each illuminated by a small light fixed to its wooden frame. The floor is linoleum made to look like white ceramic tiles, and the chairs match the picture frames. The vinyl cushions are thin and uncomfortable and do little to soften the hard seat beneath her. She drums her fingers on the armrest as she waits for her turn.

"Billie Ouellet?" a nurse calls out.

She stands, collecting her purse from its spot on the ground next to the chair leg, and follows the nurse into the doctor's office where she's weighed on a digital scale before being instructed to sit on the examination table. It's another ten-minute wait before Dr Fortin walks in, all smiles and good spirits, and he takes a seat on a swivel chair across from Billie.

"Well, look at you!" he half-shouts. "How have you been?"

"Umm, good, I guess?"

"Good? Not amazing? Your weigh-in shows you've already dropped sixteen pounds. That's phenomenal!"

"Yeah, sort of."

He frowns and leans back in his chair. "So, tell me, what's got you down about your success so far? If it's that you haven't lost enough, remember that this is a process, and you need to trust in it for your long-term success."

"No, I know. It actually feels a bit fast. But, umm, I think something's wrong," she admits.

"What do you mean?"

"Well, it's been two weeks since the operation and I'm still not able to keep anything down. Like, I can get water in and take the occasional sip of a protein shake, but I can't keep a full shake down yet."

"That's normal," he says, waving the air dismissively with one hand. "Your body is still adjusting to the Gastra-Sphaera GR. It's normal that you're feeling too full to eat much."

"But that's the thing, I'm *not* full," she says, in frustration. "I'm *never* full. And when I try to ingest anything, it comes back up."

"Well, you should only be drinking things right now. You're still on the liquid diet phase of this procedure. If you're trying to eat things earlier than you're supposed to—"

"I'm not! If I drink anything, from clear broth to a protein shake, I can only keep a few teaspoons down. But, even then, most of it just makes me throw up."

He nods his head before jotting something down on a paper in her file. "Anything else?"

"Well, yeah, actually. I can feel it."

"Feel what?"

"The device. I know you said some people would be able to after the surgery, but it's like this hot ball of metal in my gut. I just, I don't know. It doesn't feel right."

The doctor nods his head, jots something else down on the paper, before closing her file on the desk. He leans back in his chair, smiling, and crosses one arm over the other across his chest. "This is your first surgery, correct?" She nods. "It's normal for people in your position to get anxious after having a procedure done. The weight of the Gastra-Sphaera GR in your stomach is perfectly normal. It's only uncomfortable because it's not familiar to your body, but it will be. You just need to give it time."

"But—"

"The same goes for your hunger and not being able to keep food down. The hormone in the device uses a slow-release, and your body hasn't gotten used to it, which means you might still be hungry for another week or two until your body has had enough time to adjust to the hormone. When it comes to keeping your food down, you just had an operation done! Your stomach's going to be inflamed and sensitive where the incisions were made, and this inflammation and discomfort will be temporarily exacerbated by the weight affixed to the wall of your stomach. This is all perfectly normal."

She places a protective hand over her stomach. Her skin is numb where the cuts were made, nerves severed, and the sensation of her fingers on her body is dulled. "I know, it's just, I can't explain it. It feels like something isn't right."

He nods, patronisingly. "It doesn't feel right because you've never had to deal with this before, which is why you're having such a dramatic response to the healing process. But I promise it's perfectly normal. Just, do me a favour, and trust the process."

The voice in the back of her mind tells her to push the issue. Instead, Billie just nods.

She smiles from her seat on the bench, watching as the pigeons hop and flap around her, pecking at the scattered crumbs and French fries that have been thrown on the sidewalk by passers-by who've ignored the sign reading *Don't Feed The Birds*. They stare at her with their big eyes and bigger bodies, bold enough to take up space in such a busy park, but smart enough to move when an excited child runs at them with open arms. Two birds puff themselves up and dance around abandoned bread crust, making her laugh. The movement jostles her stomach, and she stills from the pain of it.

The Gastra-Sphaera GR feels like a brick in her stomach, threatening to squish her insides every time she moves. She leans back on the bench, stomach gurgling and her mouth watering as she thinks about the food she desperately wants. She wonders if, given enough time, she'll become like the birds: desperate for scraps and celebrating every bite she gets down. Billie sincerely hopes not.

She runs a hand through her hair, blanching when she sees how much of it has come out, tangled around her fingers. She tries to fluff up her bob, hoping the short style, curls, and extra volumizing hairspray will hide some of her baldness. Her heart hurts just thinking about the way her hair used to look, with waves and body for days. Now, it awkwardly frames her too-thin face, revealing bald patches of her pale scalp when the wind blows. She prays that isn't the case today, not when she's seeing her best friend for the first time since the procedure.

"Hey!" a familiar voice calls out from behind her. She smiles, gets to her feet—limbs heavy with the familiar feeling of constant exhaustion—and waves to her friend. "Oh my God! You look so tiny!" Florina shouts with excitement.

"Oh, uh, yeah!" Billie says, reluctant to talk about her weight loss.

"You're like, what? Half your size already?" Florina asks.

"Umm, no, not yet." *But soon*, Billie tells herself with dread.

"You look so good. *So good.* I can't believe I've been sitting on my ass, letting myself go in a shitty office, and you've been living your best life looking hot as fuck."

"I don't know if I'd say that," Billie admits.

She's been off work since the surgery. Although the Gastra-Sphaera GR procedure promised a speedy recovery time, with patients being able to return to work in as little as three days, Alfie had convinced her to take a leave of absence from the library for the summer so she could "focus on making sustainable changes." She suspected that what he really meant was "so you can work out and tighten up any extra skin." But since the operation, she's been too exhausted to do much beyond going for light walks or sitting on their balcony. She doesn't have the energy for anything anymore. It's been almost four months since the device was implanted, and she still can't keep food down. Although Billie is now able to keep *most* of her protein shakes down, she has to drink them throughout the day and can't take big sips without becoming nauseated. To make matters even more frustrating, she has to water them down, otherwise the thick powder and milk makes her throw up.

"I would! You look incredible!"

"Oh, well, thanks."

"Don't mention it," Florina says, looking her friend up and down with an impressed smile. "So, are you in the mood for coffee? Lunch? Both? Like, are you hungry?"

Yes, Billie thinks desperately. She's ravenous, and she misses the taste of solid food. Her stomach is weighed down and filled up by Gastra-Sphaera GR, but it does nothing to satiate her desire to eat.

"Maybe just a coffee for me," she says with a forced smile, wanting to cry.

The two of them make their way down the block. Billie asks her friend to walk slowly so that she can enjoy the sights, not wanting to admit that she's tired and badly in need of protein. When they get there, Billie waits impatiently in line as she eyes one of the small tables out on the coffee shop's patio.

"Hey there, what can I getcha?" the young barista asks with a smile.

"Umm," Billie pauses to look at the menu. "Can I have a latte with skim milk and no sugar, please?"

"Sure thing. Can I interest you in one of our delicious pastries today?" the barista asks, pointing to the selection in the display window.

"No, thanks."

The barista gives her the total, and she taps her card against the machine, waiting for it to beep and confirm her purchase before she waits for her drink at the end of the counter. Florina meets her at the end of the counter, holding a croissant on a small white plate as she tucks her receipt into the open mouth of her purse.

"God, you have some willpower. I can never say no to their baked goods. It's why I have an ass the size of Florida."

Billie laughs as she takes her freshly made drink off the counter, but her smile doesn't meet her eyes and she can't keep her focus off of the pastry in her friend's hand. Florina says something else, but Billie doesn't hear her and doesn't catch it when her friend repeats herself.

"Hey!" Florina says louder, and Billie jumps. "You okay?" she asks, grabbing her drink and following Billie to one of the empty tables.

"Yeah, yeah. Sorry."

"You zoned out *hard* back there. Everything alright?"

Billie stares at the croissant as Florina takes a bite, her stomach rumbling and mouth watering. She swallows her saliva and looks at her friend.

"Honestly? Not really."

"Why? What's up?"

She blows gently on her steaming drink before taking a sip. "I think something went wrong with the operation."

"What do you mean?"

"I, uh, I haven't been able to keep food down since they put the thing in me, and I'm hungry all the fucking time. Like, *all* the time. It wakes me up in the middle of the night and makes me want to scream."

"So just eat something."

"I *can't*. I literally can't. That's what I'm saying. Everything, *everything* comes back up. My stomach can't handle it. Like, I tried making myself soup the other night and after a few spoonfuls it was like a scene from the fucking *Exorcist*," she admits, voice hitching in her throat. "I keep staring into my fridge and wanting to eat everything in sight, but know that I'll fucking puke it up. It's bad, and I'm really worried. Alfie doesn't seem to think anything's wrong. He just keeps telling me to wait for my six-month follow-up. But like, he only cares about me being skinny. I wouldn't have even gone through with this stupid fucking thing if it wasn't for him."

She touches her stomach and her muscles clench from hunger, the weight of the Gastra-Sphaera GR a constant reminder of her decision. Everyone promised this operation would give her better health, a better body, a better life. While she'd never believed their fatphobic promises, she had believed Alfie when he said that the surgery would fix their relationship. But like all the other promises that had been made to her, this one was empty, too.

"Look," Florina says, gulping down the last of her pastry, "I know this isn't what you want to hear, but I think some of this might all be in your head."

"What?"

"Well, just, my friend's friend had the surgery, and *she* was fine. She went through a pretty similar thing where she couldn't keep the food down for a while, but like, it was fine after a few months. I think your body's probably still adjusting to everything and it'll work itself out, but you're so worried about this operation that the stress is making your symptoms seem worse to you than they really are, you know?

Like, I don't want to say you're being a hypochondriac, but like, you kind of are."

Billie takes another sip of her drink, feeling more alone than she ever has. "Yeah, uh, maybe you're right."

"I'm definitely right. Like, you look *so* beautiful right now. And, besides," she laughs, "just think of all the clothes you can afford now that you don't need food."

She holds onto the side of the toilet, stomach clenching and throat burning as the food makes its way back up her throat. She hates the acidic and rancid taste of bile and the feeling of half-eaten foods as they creep back up her oesophagus. The vomit hits the water but is drowned out by the noise of coughing. When she's finally done, she rinses her mouth with clean water from the bottle next to her on the ground, spits it into the bowl too, and flushes.

Billie leans across the bathroom floor, finding the glass Corningware dish with the leftover chicken inside, and puts the red lid back on top of it. She mentally crosses "leftover fajitas" off her list, before picking the next one to try. She eyes a Tupperware with beef stew and pops the lid off, taking a small bite of potato and carrot. She chews it until it's practically paste and swallows, hoping it will stay down, but it doesn't take long for her body to disappoint her. She runs back to the toilet and heaves, stomach aching.

"What the fuck is this?" Alfie shouts from the doorway. She hadn't mentioned her plans to experiment with solid food when he left for work in the morning. She'd wrongly assumed she'd have found something her body could keep down before he got home.

She doesn't get a chance to turn and answer him as her body forces bile out through her mouth, but she can imagine his surprise. The bathroom is full of leftovers, boxes from the cupboard, and even some frozen foods taken out of the deep freeze. Plastic cutlery lies abandoned on the ground and counters, forgotten the moment Billie's body rebelled against her.

"Sorry," she says, exhausted, spitting the last of it into the water. "I'll clean everything up, I promise."

"What the fuck are you even doing?"

She rests the side of her face against her arm, which is draped over the bowl. It's bony and uncomfortable, but she's too tired to care.

"Trying to keep something, *anything*, down. I'm so fucking hungry."

"So then you drink a protein shake! You don't binge like this!"

"I'm not bingeing, I'm testing out which foods agree with me. So far none of them do." Her stomach is sore from hours of heaving, but it's the pain of the Gastra-Sphaera GR fixed like a hot ball of lead to the inside of her body that she can't stop focusing on. "I hate this. I'm miserable. I want this fucking thing out."

"Don't be dramatic."

She finally looks up at him with a glare. "What the fuck did you say?"

"I said 'don't be dramatic'. Without the Gastra you'd still be fat. Now, you're thin and gorgeous and you have your life back. You just need to give your body time to adjust to the hormones and trust the process. But apparently," he gestures to the food around the room, "you'd rather throw all your progress away."

"Progress? Is that what you're calling it?" she says, voice echoing in the porcelain bowl.

"What else would you ca—"

"I'm fucking starving!" she shouts. "I'm hungry *all the time* and nobody cares! It's been five months since I ate anything solid. I'm *hungry*! I'm in pain *all the time*. My stomach is on fucking fire because of this Gastra. I hate it! And you're telling me I'm dramatic because I'm upset?"

He rolls his eyes. "If you really felt this way, you should have said something about it."

"That's *all* I've been doing!" she screams. "But you're not fucking listening. I hate this fucking implant. I regret getting it done."

I regret listening to you.

She doesn't say it, but the thought hangs heavy in the air between them.

"Then if that's how you really feel," he finally says as he turns on his heel to walk away, "you should tell Dr Fortin."

She listens to his footsteps as he heads back down the hall, the floor hard and uncomfortable under her sharp knees and thin skin, and closes her eyes as she catches her breath.

She looks at herself through the front-facing camera on her cell phone, her stomach sinking at the sight of her reflection. She'd applied concealer and a thick layer of foundation before she left the house, but apparently it hadn't been enough to cover the dark circles under her eyes or the hollowness of her cheeks. Her blue dress is too big and hangs awkwardly on her too-small frame. It used to be skin tight. She plays with her hair, trying to hide the ever-growing bald patches that show through her locks, but it's pointless. She puts the phone away and waits for her turn.

"Billie Ouellet?" the nurse calls.

She gets to her feet, the process taking longer than it should, and follows the woman into the doctor's office. Her steps are slow and laboured, like she's moving through pudding, and all she wants to do is lie down for a nap. She lets the woman weigh her before taking a seat on the examination table.

"Well, look at you!" Dr Fortin beams, closing the door behind him and taking a seat across from her on the chair. "You're looking so good!"

"Don't."

"Excuse me?"

"Don't lie to me. I look like shit. I'm going bald, my gums are fucking receding from all the vomiting I've done. I can see my ribs and my spine and the fucking divots in my hips. Did you know hips had divots? Because I didn't. But *now* I can fucking measure them. I'm miserable. I want it out."

He opens her file and looks at the notes. "Wow, you're down—"

"One-hundred and sixty-three pounds," she finishes for him. "That's sixty pounds more than you wanted me to lose, and one-hundred and sixty-three pounds more than *I* wanted to. I want it out."

"You want—"

"It. Out," she enunciates slowly. "The Gastra, I want it out. I want it out."

"And what makes you feel this way?"

"I can't eat anything. I can't keep—"

"You knew that portion control was going to be a huge part of the process. Wanting to eat more than you should—"

"I can't eat *anything*. I can't keep it down. I can't eat so much as a fucking steamed carrot without my body violently expelling it from me. And I'm hungry, *so* hungry all the time. Day and night, my stomach is in pain and I'm desperate to eat. But I can't. It's like torture. I've been drinking protein shakes, but they're still coming up if I have too much, or if it's too thick, or if I drink it too fast. I'm miserable. I hate this. *Please*, I need you to take this thing out. It's killing me."

He clicks his tongue against his front teeth, frowning as he flips through her file. "I understand that this has been hard on you. Adjusting to life after bariatric surgery can be tough, and the lifestyle change can be really jarring for some patients, so I get how this has been a struggle for you, I do." He pauses, trying to find a delicate way to word things. "But I also remember you coming to me when you had your stitches taken out and, uh, *exaggerating* a bit, then, too. I think you want this operation to seem harder on you than it actually is because you're looking for an easy way out. And, quite frankly, I don't want to see you undo all your progress because you're a little bit hungry, or feeling too lazy to work out, or because you want to slip into unhealthy habits again. Think about how disappointed you'll be—how disappointed your husband will be—if I let you give up on yourself. So, no, I won't be recommending that we move forward with removing the Gastra-Sphaera GR right now, but if you feel this way at your nine-month follow-up, then we can revisit the idea."

She stares at him in disbelief.

"You just need to trust the process. Okay?"

He doesn't wait for her to answer and instead continues talking.

She doesn't hear him, though. It's like cotton has been stuffed into her ears, or like she's wearing headphones with static blaring in them. All she hears is white noise and the sound of her heart pounding against her ribcage. She doesn't remember the appointment ending, getting into her car, or driving home. And yet, she's aware of herself as she throws her keys on the entranceway table and drops her purse on the rug by the door. She doesn't bother taking her shoes off as she walks into her home, tracking dirt through the hall to the kitchen. She stops in front of the fridge, opens the doors, and looks inside.

Her stomach burns, aching with both hunger and from the weight of the Gastra-Sphaera GR inside of her. She puts her hands on her skin, feeling the hollowness of her body and the bones that stick out from beneath her flesh. She's a skeleton with a pulse, a ghost with a body, a memory of who she used to be. She trails her fingers over her abdomen and stops.

At first, she thinks she's imagining things, that the hunger and emotional exhaustion have gotten to her. But when she runs her hand over her stomach again, she knows she's not crazy: she can feel the Gastra through her skin. She pulls off her dress, letting it fall to the ground, and looks at her stomach. It's concave, except for a small patch that bulges outwards. She pushes her fingers harder against her body, feeling the contour and solidness of the spherical object pushing back from inside her. She hates the device. She hates that it's ruined her life, that it's killing her slowly. She pushes against the Gastra until her nails dig into her waxen skin and come away bloody.

Her stomach growls as her hunger grows.

She looks around the kitchen, fighting through brain fog to figure out which drawer she needs, stumbling unsteadily towards it when she finally remembers. She digs through the drawer, looking for the right tool, and takes out the expensive carving knife she got as a wedding gift. She crosses the room to the dining set, pulls out a chair, and falls into it. She slumps in the seat, making sure she can clearly see the bulge under her skin before she starts.

She pinches the Gastra-Sphaera GR through her skin, steadying it, before taking the knife and pressing it against her skin. She pushes the tip in near her navel and pulls it towards her in a steady motion. Her flesh splits and blood runs out, but she doesn't see the purple shell of the device. She clenches her jaw and repositions the knife, stomach howling with hunger, and she pushes deeper as she retraces the first cut. There's an audible scraping of the metal against a hard surface and she smiles. She lets the knife fall out of her hand and onto the ground before reaching into the incision and gripping the Gastra-Sphaera GR with her bare hand. She pulls, smiling as she hears the wet tearing of the device being unsewn from her stomach. She loses her grip, the wet device slippery in her hand, and exhales with frustration. She plunges her fingers back into the wound, makes a fist around the Gastra, and gives it one more hard pull.

With a loud squelch, it pops out.

Billie rolls it between her fingers, looking at the purple sphere, still heavy with solution, and tosses it onto the table. It rolls off the edge and onto the floor, but she doesn't bother to pick it up. She's given it enough of her attention and refuses to give it a second more.

She gets up out of the wooden chair and makes her way across the room, her hunger propelling her forward, taking care not to slip in the blood that coats her legs and drips onto the floor. She opens the fridge and pulls out the first Tupperware she sees, rips the lid off, and shovels a handful of the food into her mouth. She chews fast and swallows, relief washing over her when the food doesn't come back up.

She doesn't notice the masticated chicken as it spills out of the wound in her abdomen or the splatter of it hitting the tile.

She just smiles and takes another bite.

CAITLIN MARCEAU is an author and lecturer living and working in Montreal. She holds a B.A. in Creative Writing, is a member of both the Horror Writers Association and the Quebec Writers' Federation, and spends most of her time writing horror and experimental fiction. She's been published for journalism and poetry, as well as creative non-fiction, and has spoken about horror literature at several Canadian conventions. Her collections, A Blackness Absolute *and* Palimpsest, *are slated for publication by D&T Publishing LLC and Ghost Orchid Press in 2022, respectively. If she's not covered in ink or wading through stacks of paper, you can find her ranting about issues in pop culture or nerding out over a good book. For more, check out CaitlinMarceau.ca.*

MILK

Sally Hughes

"Ma... Ma...."

Jen jolts upright, and the baby is dislodged. The gummy mouth opens wide in a silent scream. Wincing, Jen places it back on her nipple, bracing herself for the tightening pain. She must have been dozing, because she has heard it again: the voice of the child calling for its mother. The dread, fermenting in her stomach since labour, bubbles up her throat. She is suddenly cold, and pulls her dressing gown up over her shoulders, tucking the baby inside its fusty folds.

Just you and me, she thinks. *Just you and me*.

Matthew had returned from the hospital four hours ago, stripping his clothes off at the door and stepping straight into a hot shower. Once clean, he took the baby and told Jen to go to bed. After an hour of the baby screaming for her, Jen gave up on trying to sleep. The baby fed lustily, angrily, as Matthew went into their bedroom and closed the door.

Jen leans back into the sofa, for once glad of the heat of the baby on her chest. The green light of the baby monitor glows in the shadows beside the dark television. She keeps it switched on to tell herself that a day will come when it is necessary; when the baby will sleep without being held. The room is deathly still; the only sound the gurgling of blood-stained milk draining out of Jen's cracked and exhausted body.

It is so quiet here, always. Even in the middle of the day, when everyone should be at home—yelling at their children, opening wine at four o'clock—no sound reaches their apartment. The inhabitants of the building are like little ghosts; the only traces of their presence the disappearing echo of closing doors, footsteps on the stairwell. For hours, Jen hears nothing beyond the baby's yells and her own imaginings.

"Ma?"

For one moment, the light on the monitor zooms up to red.

The same voice. But Jen is not dreaming. She is awake, wide awake. Holding the baby in place with both hands, she rises and walks towards the monitor. It looks blank, its steady light a sign that all is well. But she heard it.

She saw it.

She crouches down awkwardly, so close that she can see the faint flickering of the green light, hear the whispers of static from the speaker. She puts her ear up to the white plastic.

Immediately, as if it has been waiting for her to draw near, the voice thunders through the monitor: "Milk, Ma! Milk."

Jen falls backwards, jarring her back on the sharp edge of the coffee table, biting down a cry. She looks wildly around the empty room. Is it Matthew, making some kind of joke? He has been under a huge amount of pressure, working in unimaginable circumstances—

but she already knows it is not Matthew. He could not make his voice that young, that broken, that hungry.

She waits for the voice to come again, but there is only silence. Balancing the baby against her shoulder, Jen lunges forward and yanks the monitor's plug out of the wall. The green light fades slowly.

Still silence.

In the bedroom, Matthew lies motionless as stone. The monitor here is flashing, beeping softly, knowing that its twin is lost. Jen switches it off, then puts the baby in the Moses basket. It shifts and croaks, looking for her. Jen lies down, extends one hand to put her index finger in the tiny mouth. Immediately it quietens, suckles.

Jen lies still and listens for the voice to come again. In the stagnant darkness she hears only the thrum of her heart, the soft slurp of the baby.

There must be at least half a dozen children living in this building, all plugged into tablets and laptops. Jen imagines a spider's web of Wi-Fi snaking through the thick walls and floors. Perhaps it was only a voice from another apartment, caught on that network and captured for a moment on the monitor.

Perhaps that is what the voice has always been.

"You need sleep, that's all." The health visitor's face is frozen in an unflattering grimace. "Is Matthew still—?"

"He's working nights. When he is home, he's exhausted."

The woman's features shudder and jump and finally catch up with the steady, tinny voice. "It must be hell right now. What about your mum? Is there any way she can help?"

Jen shakes her head. "She's up in Edinburgh with my sister."

The health visitor shrugs. There's nothing to be done, not with things as they are. "Try to sleep when the baby does," she says, lamely. "This stage won't last forever. Soon you'll be able to get into a rhythm, a routine. Then it will be easier. And don't worry about the bleeding. For some women it can carry on for six, even eight weeks."

"I know… it's just the feeding is painful still."

"You must expect some tenderness at first."

At first. Jen has been doing this for over 600 hours.

"It's very painful," she says.

"Are you using the cream I recommended?"

"Yes, every time I feed." She has to, to be able to endure the moment when the tight little mouth grips on to her.

"Might be an idea to lay off it for a while. It can keep the nipples soft, you see, when they need to toughen up."

Jen switches off the laptop. The small white light of the webcam reminds her of the baby monitor, unplugged and hidden in the shadows and dust beneath the TV cabinet. Matthew is sleeping. He will wake in a couple of hours, shower and eat and then leave for the hospital. She could take the baby for a walk before he wakes up—the sunshine is gleaming on the roofs of the parked cars outside. Her phone pings. It's an email from the health visitor with a pdf attached: *Coronavirus: Parent Information for Newbern Babies*.

They could go and sit in the communal garden. But the garden is tucked behind the building, always damp and cold, even in midsummer.

She has never liked this place, not ever. Matthew said it was perfect—*perfect*—for a woman working on the radical political lives of the female mill workforce. She thought the flat overpriced and soulless. What she disliked most was the way every surface had been made smooth and shiny and sweet-smelling. As though people hadn't laboured their lives away here, as though children hadn't died here. She finds herself thinking of them a lot during the dead hours, when she sponges excrement off the baby's kicking, gleaming limbs: the children whose lives had been offered up for a twist of thread, a roll of worsted.

Jen only feels truly at rest in houses with no history. She can cope with the horrors of the past when they are contained within perfectly catalogued box files, shelved on stacks that she can leave at the end of the day. Here, she can read them in every brick, every inch of glass, and no amount of Farrow & Ball paint can obscure them. In her work, she tries to recover what is vital, admirable, out of the past. Here, she only feels caught in its terrors.

When did she first hear the voice? She can't remember now. Perhaps it was even before the baby came. She had been working hard, too late on, trying to finish a draft of a paper. After she climbed the valley side to the neat churchyard and found the gravestone marking all the parish orphans who had died in this mill, the huge monolith began to haunt her dreams. She would wake up weeping after enduring a chorus of lost children crying for their mothers. When she talked to Matthew, he said it was anxiety about the birth, anxiety about the virus. Then in April things got so bad that she really was frightened for him, frightened every time he left for work, frightened every time he sneezed, and she didn't want to worry him by telling him the dreams had got worse, begun leeching into her waking life, as they had since they brought the baby home.

Jen looks down at the baby, wet pink mouth open and drooling. Even sleeping, it looks hungry. The baby has no history. It is brand new. But its hunger feels ancient and angry.

Two hours until a feed and the milk has already saturated her breast pads, soaked into her bra. She feels a stir in her bowels and squeezes down hard. If she leaves the baby to go to the toilet, it will wake up and cry and the only way to soothe it will be with her fragile, bleeding nipples.

They all say she is doing so well: the health visitor; Matthew's parents. You're doing so well. You're a natural mother.

She does not want to hear it. She just wants someone to say, you've done enough now.

But they never do.

At eight o'clock, the residents go out onto their balconies and decking to clap and cheer. The baby fusses at her shoulder as Jen opens up the French doors, walks outside to listen. There is a soft, warm sunset glowing somewhere above; down here in the valley, it is lost in shadows.

Jen thought she was eager for the sight and sound of other humans, but she feels an unexpected surge of disgust at the sight of the grinning faces across the courtyard, the rainbows in the windows. When she met someone on the stairs they smiled and said, nice to have your husband home for the early months, lockdown's good for something. Oh yes, she wants to say. You clap for carers and have no idea Matthew's the one who'll look after you if you get ill.

Telling herself her anger is down to hunger—she only managed one slice of toast for lunch—she closes the door on the bangs and cheers and makes herself some food. After two mouthfuls of soggy bran flakes, the baby's fusses turn to wails. Jen reaches for the donut-shaped pillow, lifts her jumper, and bites her lip as the ravenous mouth latches on. Tears start in her eyes at the ferocity of it. How can such cruelty be natural? "Gentle," she whispers, uncertain of whether she speaks to the baby or herself. "Gentle."

The clapping and whooping is muffled beneath the baby's sucking.

At the sudden, shrill whistle, Jen springs up, clutching the baby to her chest. The noise is deafening, pushing at her eardrums, echoing through her head. She wants to press her hands against her ears to keep it out, but she cannot let go of the baby. The whistle screams on for an unbearable minute, and as it fades, there is a thundering of feet, as if a thousand people are running for their lives. Could it have been a fire alarm? Jen staggers to the front door, the clattering roar only inches away, and opens it into an empty corridor. She blinks, unable to make sense of what she sees, for she can still hear the clanking footsteps, the banging of wooden clogs against cold flagstone floors.

The baby is entangled in her jumper, utterly furious, its mouth searching in vain for her flesh. Jen lets it cry on, as her bewilderment slides into an awful, deadening fear.

The footsteps are fading now, clicking away around the corner to the damp stairwell. And then there is only the outraged squeaking of the baby, and Jen's own ragged breath.

The baby is ravenous, its body shaking with an appetite that seems beyond human, but Jen is empty. She walks up and down the flat with the baby on her shoulder, rubbing its back, patting its nappy-cushioned bottom. The crying is so loud that Jen takes out her sore breasts in despair, but it is useless. After a second's frantic sucking, the baby comes off, howling, inconsolable.

She looks at the clock. Matthew doesn't finish work for another five hours. She puts the baby down in their bedroom and shuts the door. The outraged shouts of misery are barely dampened. They must be keeping everyone in the building awake.

Jen knows, clearly and certainly, that she is failing.

Her fingers shake as she finds the number on her phone. She cannot keep the sobs out of her voice as she speaks.

"I'm sorry—I shouldn't be calling, it's so late. It's just—I don't know what to do. I don't know what to do!"

"It's okay, love." The voice on the other end of the phone is calm, unflustered. "There's always someone awake here. Tell me what's wrong."

Jen remembers this voice from her delivery. It had called her back into her body, back into the pain and the fear. "I can hear you screaming from down the hall," it had barked. "Stop screaming and start pushing!"

But afterwards, when Jen had lain broken and stunned, the baby on her chest, it had been gentle. It is gentle now—silent as Jen blurts out incoherent sentences while the baby cries. *It's so hungry, so hungry, and I don't have enough. Do I need to give formula? Please, can't I give formula?*

"You've done the right thing to call us," the voice says, as soothing as a blank page, an empty calendar. "The baby's, what, four weeks old now? It's a growth spurt. They do need more at this time, but don't worry, it won't last. And you've got enough, trust me. You've got enough…"

Jen tries to listen to the voice, but the baby's cries are so loud. She opens the French doors and walks out on to the balcony. The soft night air dries the tears on her cheeks to a sticky crust of salt. The moon hangs low, cold and blue.

"So many mums call us at this time," the voice in her ear says. "You're not alone…"

Jen hears a sound from inside the flat. An alien noise that shouldn't be there: a shuffling, an irregular thump.

For a second, she cannot move. Then she cuts off the kindly voice with a flick of her finger, and, mouth twisted, walks back into the stuffy air of the living room. It is empty. The remains of the curry Matthew had made that afternoon still curdle in the wok on the greasy cooker. One corner of a yellowed linen square dangles out of the washing machine drum.

Thump… thump… thump…

She can almost trace the noise with her staring eyes as it crosses in front of her, moves towards the closed bedroom door.

And then the baby is suddenly, abruptly, silent.

Jen drops her phone. It hits the floorboards and breaks apart, landing in three flat, apologetic pieces.

Jen skids to the bedroom, wrenches open the door. In the reflected light from the living room, she can see that the baby has turned itself over and lies face down in the basket. A wisp of dark hair lies like a shadow above the angry red neck.

Jen is too frightened to cry as she falls on the baby and presses it to herself, inhaling the sickly-sweet smell of curdled milk. In the moment before the baby squeaks and jerks and slams its head against her chin, Jen is sure she hears a strange, thick breathing coming from somewhere behind her.

Matthew runs her a deep, warm bath, with lavender oil. Jen lowers herself in, flinching at the sting of hot water against her stitches. He has had two full days off, and in his large, gentle presence the voices are silent. Jen even got a little sleep during the thin, light hours of early morning. But Matthew goes back to the ward this afternoon. She can hear him trying to distract the baby from her absence, singing the only songs he knows all the words to: Pearl Jam, Faith No More, Iron Maiden.

Jen has not drunk enough and feels the beginnings of a headache throbbing behind her right eye. She sinks under the filmy surface, where it is warm and silent, feeling the pulse of blood through her temples, the touch of cold on her knees. She stays under for as long as she can, lying in the blank darkness that exists where the baby is not.

When she re-emerges, gasping for air, the singing has stopped. The high, wailing cry cuts through the heavy, floral fug. Jen feels the familiar prickling tingle, and grey milk drips into the cloudy water.

The baby fed well at teatime, and lolled in her arms afterwards, a warm bag of flour. Jen was bold enough to lie it down next to her on the sofa, and this is permissible as long as she leaves her hand on the rounded, rippling tummy. Jen's head is getting worse. She flicks through repeats of American sitcoms while the pressure builds behind her eye. Finally, it all becomes too much, and she switches the telly off. Her hand still on the baby, her head rolls forward. In the fading golden evening, she sleeps.

She is awoken by a juddering rumble. At first she thinks it is her headache, turned massive and monstrous; then, as she struggles to wakefulness, she realises it is something else, something that cannot possibly come from her head. The whole apartment is shuddering, as if some colossal machine grinds deep in the bowels of the building. It is swelteringly hot and Jen feels the bristle of sweat on her neck. The air is limpid, cloudy. She rubs hard at her eyes with the heel of her hand and looks again, to see a mass of softly drifting fibres glinting in the slanting light of the setting sun.

Jen sucks in a breath and coughs it out. The air feels thick and sticky in her lungs. The baby still sleeps, a thin dusting of fluff on its glistening cheeks. Jen catches it up clumsily, presses it under her clammy chin as she gets to her feet.

Then, with hideous clarity, she hears what she has been listening for.

A voice calling for comfort.

"Milk, Ma! Milk."

A thump and scrape.

"Please, Ma. *Milk.*"

A gasping, desperate whisper.

Jen does not move. Her heart pounds against her ribs. The baby squirms, rammed too tight against her collarbone.

Another scrape, another thud. It is close now. It is right behind them.

Jen stumbles to the French doors, where she turns, half blinded by the sun. There is something there, in the shadows behind the sofa—a thin, ragged, yellow, starving something. It comes towards her, dragging one leg behind its tiny trunk, the rough wooden clogs scraping painfully against their polished oak floors. Its filthy pinafore is torn and shows one purple, twisted kneecap, facing the wrong way.

"Ma," it says. Two broken teeth jut at the front of the yawning pink mouth. "Milk, Ma. *Milk*."

"I am not your mother," Jen whispers, clutching the baby tighter. But she feels her treacherous nipples tighten and release. Her milk flows.

The thing takes another jerking step forward. "I am not your mother!" Jen shrieks, and then, as the thing reaches her, grasps for her, she feels the baby fall from her hands.

Matthew finds her an hour later in the gleaming, empty corridor. Her voice is hoarse from calling, her fingernails bloody and ragged from scratching at the locked front door. One swollen breast hangs out of her grubby dressing gown, and a dribble of milk soils the shining granite floor.

Jen's arms are empty. Behind the door, the flat is silent, as if there is no baby in there at all.

"I'm so glad to see you in person," the health visitor says. In her plastic pinny and mask, she looks like something from a Kate Bush video. "I was worried about you after we spoke. But I can see just by looking at you that you're both doing beautifully."

Matthew squeezes Jen's free hand as she cradles the baby. After rescuing their child, cold and sleepy, from the floor of the apartment, he phoned his supervisor. She agreed he could take his two weeks deferred paternity leave immediately. Then he made up a bottle with their emergency supply of formula. Only after the baby was settled did he hold Jen as she rocked and trembled. She could still see that thing in the room, hear it crying out for milk, feel it pressing its broken mouth into her flesh.

When she did sleep, exhaustion wiped her dreams clean, and she woke after six blank hours, with breasts groaning to feed.

She hadn't been doing enough, Matthew told her that morning as she nursed the baby. Her brain was going into overdrive. She needed to be able to read, to think, to write. But he was here now. He would help her.

"We've decided to introduce a formula feed," he says to the health visitor. "Perhaps before bed. So Jen can get a little more sleep."

The woman exhales, and Jen is glad she can't see the expression behind the mask. "We don't recommend that – not for at least six months. And Isobel has been gaining weight so well, just with breast milk alone," she says.

Matthew looks at Jen. "Feeding is still very painful," he says.

"Can I have a look at how Isobel is latching on?" the health visitor asks. "It shouldn't be painful if she's on properly. I might be able to help."

Jen obediently unbuttons her shirt and lifts her vest as the midwife shifts closer.

There is a sharp intake of breath.

Jen looks down.

Her left breast is branded in bruises of red and pink. A circle of angry crimson surrounds the nipple. And, within the circle, two deep purple lines, edged in yellow. The marks of two teeth, gauged into her body.

In the stunned silence, the baby sneezes, then opens its mouth wide, in a gummy, wet smile.

SALLY HUGHES lives in the Scottish Highlands and works as a library supervisor. She has a PhD in literature, and is currently seeking representation for her first novel, a Gothic mystery set in 1860s Yorkshire. She tweets at @sallyhbooks.

IT WON'T BE SO BAD

Varian Ross

She had been created for someone who did not want her. She had been named Lilly because it was the old name her flesh and blood counterpart had once used. For every change her counterpart willingly made to their body, Lilly was changed further. When Monica cut their hair short, Lilly was whisked away and given longer, thicker hair. When they began to bind their chest on the regular, Lilly was given larger breasts.

Then her counterpart skipped their period by a week. And Lilly was forced to go through the greatest change of all. She knew it was much too fast. In a human, this took months. But one day she woke—as much as an AI could wake—to a belly distended and swollen. And a knowing that something would be pouring out of her soon. Something her counterpart did not want.

It would be a party, Lilly thought. There would be guests. So many others watching as she went through the most painful thing anyone could go through. She felt a simulated kick low in her body. If she'd had the ability, she would have cringed.

Neither Lilly nor her counterpart wanted this. It was all the others who wanted to see this happen. All the others who wanted to prove that it wouldn't be so bad.

She had been strapped to the passenger seat of the van. The party planners were talking excitedly about the cake they were bringing. The red velvet with white frosting. While Lilly thrashed and moaned through a mouth stitched closed, they would be eating cake and laughing. Those around her would not have a care in the world.

The van slowed, then stopped. Lilly's straps were unbuckled, and she was picked up. She could still walk, but she had no voice to protest with. They all thought she was far too delicate in her condition.

A cramp deep inside her made her flinch. There was a chuckle from the woman who carried her.

"It'll be over before you know it." A door closed behind them. Lilly could hear voices and laughter. "Once Monica sees how easy it is, they'll want one of their own."

The first time Monica had seen a Replica give birth, they had hidden. They had fled into the bathroom. They had stood in the stall, shaking, unable to name why they were so upset. They didn't understand how this could all happen so… calmly. How all the adults could stand around and make small talk. How the grown-ups could eat cake while in the same room, a Replica of the expecting mother strained to bring new life into the world.

Now their own replica was being placed on that same table. Despite their hypothetical pregnancy not even being confirmed, their family had been so quick to assume. To set up a party. To not even wait a week and see if Monica's period was just late. That's what happened—they were bleeding even as they started down at a Replica of their own naked body. This was what others saw them as—this body was missing the scar from riding bikes down a bumpy forest path and taking a nasty fall. The hair was too long, the breasts too full. Above all, the stomach was much too swollen. It looked ready to burst. There was no way this had developed over the natural time it took for a child to grow.

A Replica was meant to be a preview of what was to come, to see what changes needed to be made to a birthing plan. Monica had no such plan. They had no need for a plan like that. Their partner wasn't interested in the activities that could lead to a child, and Monica respected her for that. In their relationship, Monica felt freedom from the pressure of "accidents", as their family so coyly put it.

"It should be starting soon." The nurse—who was there to answer any questions—smiled at Monica. "You'll see, it's easy."

At her words, the Replica gave a jerk. It turned its head from side to side, looking at those who stood around it. Its pale green eyes shone with fear. Its back lifted as a contraction rolled through it.

"It doesn't really feel fear or pain, don't worry. This is just a simulation," the nurse said with a smile. "Shall we go have some cake?"

Waves of pain tore through Lilly. She felt her back arch to the point she feared it would crack in two. As the contraction ended, she slammed back down on the table. Another burst of pain as she made sudden contact with the cold metal.

"You're in for it," she heard someone in the crowd of guests say. "I don't think I've seen a Replica labour this hard before. They normally don't thrash around like that."

The wires holding Lilly's mouth closed began to crack. She strained to open her mouth, to scream at them all. To scream that neither she nor Monica wanted this.

Monica was frozen with a piece of cake in their hand. The red velvet was moist and dripping frosting. Their eyes were wide, watching Lilly. The expression on their face was nothing but fear.

"Now you see, it's not bad at all." A woman wearing pearls stood behind Monica. "Eat your cake, dear. I made it special for the occasion."

Lilly threw her head back as another spasm wracked her body. She felt the wires finally break. The metal cracked, tiny shards sticking in her throat.

"You won't start smoking," the woman in pearls said to Monica. "You'll have one of your own someday, don't worry."

Lilly's screams filled the air, and smoke came pouring from her throat.

Monica stared at the table, their cake forgotten. Were they the only one who saw something wrong? The nurse did not look at the Replica oddly, even as the wires holding its mouth closed suddenly snapped. Tiny shards of metal sprayed over the Replica's body. Its mechanical screams pierced the air. Its body thrashed and heaved. But even as it strained, only blood and mucus poured out from between its legs.

"It's not in pain," the nurse said as Monica approached the Replica. "As I said earlier, it's only a simulation—"

"KILL. ME." The Replica's words tore through the air. Its body contorted as waves of pain lashed through it. "I DON'T. WANT THIS."

"Now, don't get hysterical." The nurse stepped forward and ran a hand through the Replica's hair. She hauled the Replica to its knees. "Gravity will help with the baby."

"NOTHING. INSIDE ME. BUT STONE." Between the words, the Replica strained, pushing harder. It doubled over, wailing. Its lower back split open, wires exposed for all the world to see.

The nurse bent over. She reached between the Replica's legs. She withdrew her hand, nodding even as her patient howled with waves of agony.

"Everything is on schedule," she said to Monica, with a bright smile.

As she spoke those words, the Replica's body began to split in two. The crack in the skin rose upward. Now the wires and metal could be seen in the Replica's stomach. It fell backwards into a reclining position. It still continued to push, the movement unstoppable.

"You'll need some pain medicine," a guest said at Monica's shoulder. "But someday you'll have an accident and be so happy."

On the table, the crack in the Replica's body continued to grow.

Lilly was being split in two. The pain of exposed wires hitting the air only added to the agony of the simulated birth. She felt the tear rip up through her stomach. It was nearly at her heart now. Still, no one was doing anything. No one was knocking her out, cutting her open, and removing the stone that was causing all this.

"ALL. YOUR. FAULT." Her words echoed. Still, the guests around the room laughed and ate cake. They did not listen to her. No one offered even a comforting hug. Another wave of pressure forced her to bear down and double over. As Lilly straightened, she felt the split reach her heart.

She did not know if the agony that shot through her veins was the birth finally progressing. Or if it was her robotic heart being exposed to air. She looked to the nurse, who was supposed to help her.

How long had she been like this, nothing but a vessel for pain?

But the nurse only shoved a hand in the gaping hole between her legs. She turned to Monica. She said the child—she had not believed Lilly's words about it turning to stone—must be stuck. But all it would take was a little more pushing. Not to worry.

Monica stepped forward. The nurse must have been telling them that Lilly could not understand them, because they turned back and glared at the woman in the scrubs. Lilly could not hear what they were saying beneath the pain her world had become.

But she could feel Monica's fingers as they closed around her heart. This time the pain was welcome.

"PLEASE." Lilly hoped Monica could hear the relief in her voice. "THEY MADE ME. I CAN'T. DO THIS."

Monica yanked hard, Lilly's heart coming out into their hands. The metal must have been burning hot. Monica yanked again, even as tears ran down their cheeks and their hands blistered. The wires severed with a final pop.

"Sure you can do it," Lilly heard a guest say as the world began to go dark. She felt her body collapse on to the table. The metal beneath her was cool now. She could still feel the thick stone lodged inside of her. It would never come out now. Not unless they cut her open.

"I'm not even pregnant," she heard Monica say. "My period was just late."

Through failing hearing, Lilly heard Monica put her heart down on the table with a clunk. The guests were silent. Either that or her hearing was gone for good.

"Don't anyone ever tell me 'It's not that bad' ever again." Monica's words were muffled. "Because that looked pretty fucking bad to me."

As the party and the guests slipped away from her awareness, Lilly silently agreed.

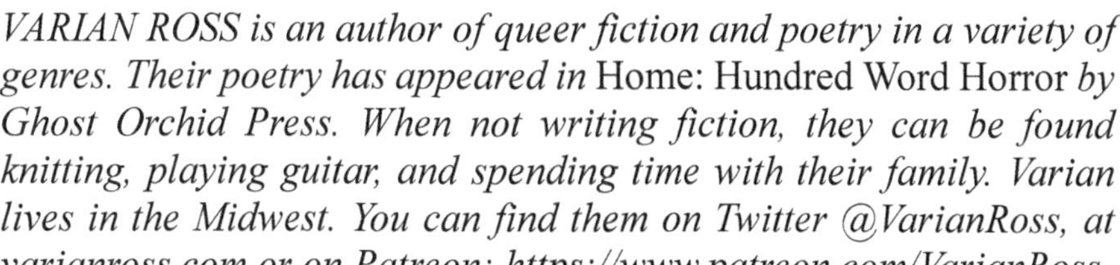

VARIAN ROSS is an author of queer fiction and poetry in a variety of genres. Their poetry has appeared in Home: Hundred Word Horror *by Ghost Orchid Press. When not writing fiction, they can be found knitting, playing guitar, and spending time with their family. Varian lives in the Midwest. You can find them on Twitter @VarianRoss, at varianross.com or on Patreon: https://www.patreon.com/VarianRoss.*

WHAT GOES DOWN, MUST COME UP

Evelyn Freeling

Here we meet again.

I'm crouched over you, my porcelain god. I don't set my knees on the ground. I'm agile. Practiced. Giddy, because I successfully created a diversion to get here. To come meet you.

I'm at dinner with my husband and brother who's visiting from out of town. An Italian joint, brother's choice. I can't help myself around pasta. My husband's a finance exec, my brother an anti-capitalist neo-hippie. I start them arguing on a tax bill in the news, so they won't notice how long I'm gone.

Now, taupe tiles under my heels, the perfume of pauperie and the leftover stench of a stranger's shit poison the air. I dance a slight shoulder jig at my stealth. My cleverness. My ability to deceive the people I love and keep up appearances simultaneously.

I'm sick.

Our meetings are brief. If this were an affair of a more illicit nature, we might call them quickies. I slide my fingers into my own wet warmth. I understand the appeal of it. Why my husband enjoys it so much. I have the spot memorised. I fiddle. The muscle there is strong after so many years of this. It resists. I make it give in. The same come-hither motion my husband occasionally makes inside of me.

It comes and you're ready to take it.

It lurches in my stomach first, acidic and gurgling. It blazes its way up, through my oesophagus and throat. It doesn't taste bad anymore. Vomit is an acquired taste. I can tell without looking which parts of the meal come up first. I can discern the olive oil from the chunks of bread. The Italian dressing on the salad. The red pepper in the marinara. My palette is well trained.

I avoid spice normally. It burns too much. Sometimes, I like the pain though. That's my answer when you ask me, "What's a girl like you doing in a place like this?"

Sometimes, I come to you for the pain.

Most times, I don't know why I come to you anymore.

I button my shirt back up. It's a white blouse and I can't afford suspicious stains. It isn't unusual to do this partially naked. I've stripped dresses off in public restrooms to keep our encounters discrete.

I clean my face. Wipe spots off of my jeans. A chunk of lettuce off of my left heel. I return to my husband and brother like nothing has happened. Like there's still so much to look forward to this evening. Like three brief minutes with you isn't the best part of my night.

My favourite thing to purge is ice cream. It tastes exactly the same coming up as it does going down. It's almost like enjoying two servings. Except for the muscles constricting and the body heaving and the deep ache in my gut afterwards. I've convinced myself that purging ice cream is okay because the dairy is a base which neutralises the acidity of the purge. Meaning, it shouldn't destroy tooth enamel. Meaning, even if I someday do end our relationship, I can always come back if it's ice cream. For the warm memories.

Like I said, I'm sick.

I'm pregnant. I lie in bed, rub my belly, swollen and bloated and nearly ready to pop. My husband's urine tinkles against your porcelain. Reminding me. I'm into my third trimester and I hardly miss you. During the first, you and I spent more time together than ever before. So much time, you and I are no longer 'we' in my mind.

If there's a time for this relationship to end, it's now. For the sake of my daughter inside me, depending on me. On my body. My love for it. I keep the bathroom door closed so I don't have to look at you every time I pass.

As my palm circles slowly around the dome of my belly, she hiccups. Her daily reminder that this sacrifice is worth so much more than my fleeting encounters with you. I tell myself this is her way of thanking me, but I'm the one who should thank her.

It's now three months since our last rendezvous. Longer still since our last meeting not coerced by nausea. The longest I've gone without you in a decade. A decade, can you believe that? This is my longest lasting relationship.

Was my longest lasting relationship. You and I are over now.

The first time I heard of bulimia I was in third grade. I picked up a Baby-Sitters Club book from the small raw pinewood shelf at the daycare I attended after school. One of the characters had it. I don't remember which one. I don't remember any of the girls. I had never read a single instalment before. I don't know why I did that day or why it happened to be that instalment.

Maybe it was fate.

I have never felt that way about my husband, but I met him online. You and I met serendipitously. I have given so much of myself to you all because of one seemingly random choice to pick up a silly book. If there's such a thing as fate, I suppose that's as close as it gets.

After I read that book, I was fascinated. I inquired with my mom, "What's bulimia?" She explained and asked why I wanted to know. I could've told her I read it in a book, but I lied. I never knew toilets could be used for such things and was ashamed of the way you left me awestruck long before I knelt down before you. Instead, I told her there was a girl in my class who threw up during school lunches.

It became a thing. Every day, my mom urged me to go to the school counsellor and report the girl. She was eight, like me. It terrified my mom that a girl so young could already be so ill. Finally, my mom did it on my behalf. The counsellor wanted a name. I gave him one I thought made sense. Someone who, to my young mind, looked like they could be coupled with an eating disorder. She was the pretty blonde in my class who all the boys ogled.

It was only third grade, and already I noticed these things. Already, I made these associations.

I collapse onto the couch and prop my feet on the coffee table, legs splayed out, unable to cross my hideously bloated ankles. "I'm exhausted," I complain to my husband. His hand is warm on my back as he pats and says, "Pregnancy is hard." We do this every night now. Feet raised, hands and forearms cupping my belly, lifting up to relieve the constant ache in my pelvis. "I'm exhausted," I whine. "Pregnancy is hard," he reminds me.

He doesn't understand.

The final weeks of pregnancy are a brutal lesson in the miracle of the pregnant body. The intestines, together nearly twenty-one feet long, squeeze into the space of a few inches, compress into the lungs. Only a little food makes me feel so full I'll burst. It's a dangerous feeling. When it comes, bugs writhe underneath my flesh. My mind blurs. My breath shallows until I'm winded. Anxiety is physical. A devil residing in my body, breaking me down, convincing me I cannot live without you.

I'm exhausted from resisting.

I want to gorge. I want to stuff my face with every piece of food in the kitchen until muscle memory kicks in and my body reflexively forces every bite back up. So far, I have resisted for my unborn child.

After my husband finishes patting me on the back, he withdraws to the kitchen. The freezer door peels open and smacks closed. He returns, something hidden behind his back, a clandestine smirk across his face. He flourishes a pint of ice cream. I dip the spoon in and eat. Leisurely. I pretend to watch whatever Netflix show we're binging. Inside my head, I count the minutes between bites. One hundred and twenty seconds between each. This is how I control myself.

It works. I don't gorge, but I don't need to. Six minutes, three bites, and already my body pleads. The anxiety is too much.

"Just this once," you say as I kneel before you, ready and willing finally.

"Just this once."

I even believe myself as I say it.

My water breaks two hours later. Four weeks and two days early. Late enough that my daughter doesn't end up in ICU, but early enough that she's considered premature. It's my fault. I don't have self-control. I never did. I hate myself for a month while her body grows before my eyes. Her skinny arms kill me. It's my fault. The doctor tells me otherwise, but I know better.

"Never again," I tell myself.

My husband and I have done it. The baby is sleeping on schedule, for six hours through the night before she needs to be fed and put back to sleep again. Four hard months and we're finally here. I take the opportunity to shower. I even shave.

With my leg propped on top of you, the razor blade in my hand, I am David, you are Goliath. Finally, I've vanquished you. Four months strong. I know you don't like this. I hear you call me at night. Beg me to go to the kitchen while my husband and baby sleep, then come to you, but I'm strong now. Motherhood has empowered me.

I slip a silk nightie over my now smooth-as-a-dolphin skin and crawl on top of my husband in our darkened bedroom. I put him in my wet warmth, where my fingers haven't played in four months. I gag as he slides all the way back. Four months and still my body readies itself for you, not him.

"Don't stop," he commands.

But I have to. I straddle him instead. He sighs. This is good, too. He watches me in the blue moonlight leaking through the window as I grind on him the way he likes. I turn it into a show. Lift the nightie, lick my fingers in slow, dramatic slurps, and touch myself. It's been ages since we last made love. He's eager. Takes control. Bounces me up and down. I close my eyes and enjoy the pounding until it makes me dizzy.

I gasp. I clasp a hand over my mouth. *No*, I think. It can't be. I'm stronger than this, but the dizziness makes me nauseous. I need to run. To you. My husband grips my hips, holds me firmly on top of him.

"Fuck," he groans.

He's almost done. I can hold it.

But I can't. I feel stomach acid burn my nose, leak out my nostrils, drizzle over the crest of my lip. *No*, I think. My last meal hurdles through me and projectiles onto him. A chunky flood pours over his chest and splatters onto our bed sheets at the same time that he finishes inside of me.

He screeches and flies off the bed without waiting for me to disembark. I fall to the floor and lie there, moaning in shame. He retches in the bathroom. The sound of his vomit splashing against you wafts through the hall into our bedroom. I tremble to him. He's on his knees, arms limp over your rim. He isn't used to this.

"What the fuck was that?" He mumbles.

I wonder the same thing.

Mr Tate, my freshman English teacher, had our class read *Go Ask Alice*. During discussion, he asked if we thought Alice had an eating disorder.

Mr Tate was a well-meaning older man, white and bald with square-rimmed glasses. He kept a record player in the classroom and liked to play us music from decades past. He was the kind of teacher who was raw and approachable, even when he got on his metaphorical soapbox. He wanted us to understand there were dangers behind small decisions like, "Just this once."

I didn't speak as the other students discussed whether Alice's behaviour with food could be classified as an eating disorder, until Mr Tate explained that eating disorders were about control. Then, I raised my hand.

"People get eating disorders to lose weight."

I insisted this relentlessly. I argued with him for nearly five minutes, until he was visibly annoyed. Until I noticed other students shooting me looks with squinted eyes and scrunched brows. Then, I shut up.

He was right. I realised that in college, when my rendezvous with you no longer coincided with feeling fat but with midterms and finals, bad grades, fights with my boyfriend. When I ate to fulfilment what's widely considered "healthy food," but feeling fulfilled at all made me ache with anxiety and I felt compelled, *forced* to turn to you.

I realised only when our relationship had already become a power struggle.

My daughter coos in the backseat. She's blossomed into a chubby little thing with black curly hair like her father's and eyes that light up when she looks at me. She fills me with a happiness I didn't know existed. It's not all good, but even the worst moments with her are infinitely better than the best moments of my life before she existed.

I glance in the rearview mirror that reflects a small round mirror hanging above her car seat. It's there so I can sneak glimpses of her while I drive. Maternity leave is over now. My days are a routine of dropping her off at daycare and anxiously watching the clock, waiting to scoop her back into my arms. Feel her tiny open mouth against my cheek in a slobbery infant kiss. It's a twenty-minute drive from the daycare to home. For forty minutes each day, the little round mirror is all I get of her gummy smile.

She giggles. Her body parts are a recent discovery. I watch in the mirror as her fingers fumble her nose and ears. She reaches into her mouth. Sticks her fingers inside. Mouths on her hand. Sticks her fingers further. She gags.

The noise freezes my blood solid.

It's not the first instance she's done this. Every time, I think it's a circular punishment. To teach me a lesson. A message to say, "See what you've been doing to yourself all these years?"

I strain behind and around the car seat, crooking my shoulder at painful angles. She cackles as I wrench her fingers from her mouth. "Don't do that!" I shout. I don't mean to raise my voice. I'm scared, but now so is she. Her face screws up and she bursts into sobs I can't calm until I stop on the side of the road, crawl into the backseat and hold her in my arms.

I ache for her to love herself like I never have. To show her body a kindness mine has never known. I don't know how to teach her these things, yet. I'll learn, though. In so many ways, mothers are birthed during labour.

The other night was a freak accident. Nothing to do with you. You did not cast a spell on me and call my husband to you out of spite. This isn't a curse my daughter is predestined to inherit. You're an inanimate object. A toilet. I'm the one with the power. That's what I tell myself. I'm different now. I have the power to choose.

It's been two days since I last ate. My breast milk is drying. My daughter is furious that I can't feed her, that I'm forcing her to switch to formula. My husband doesn't understand the transition is intentional. He doesn't see me chew and spit food into my napkin at dinner. He doesn't notice I use seven napkins at a meal now. This isn't to lose weight. This is self-control. To prevent myself from falling to my knees before you, repenting, begging your forgiveness for the time spent away.

At work, my stomach gnaws. I fill it with black coffee in the break-room. Cream or sugar would be ammunition for you. I laugh at someone's joke I don't hear and wonder what it's like to be a stranger to your torment. I'm envious of the people in my office. Men and women. Gender doesn't matter. You don't discriminate. I can't remember the last time you didn't occupy my thoughts. I can't remember what it was like to not struggle against you every second. My life is a constant fight now. This daily battle rattles me. I'm worn out.

"Ready for your presentation?"

My director beams at me. She's the kind of woman and mother I wish I was. Tall and slim in the places motherhood hasn't eviscerated. Always well styled with a red lip and a dark-haired bob that stuns against her pale skin.

These aren't the reasons I wish I was like her.

She tells me every day how wonderfully I'm doing. What a good mother I am. What a good wife. What a hard worker. How amazed she is by me. My cheeks suffuse with blood under her shower of flattery. Part of me loves it. Her positivity is infectious. I almost believe her.

The other part of me despises how good I am at fooling the people I respect and admire most. Nobody knows who I am. Only you.

When I don't answer, she pats my arm. "You're going to throw down. You always do," she reassures me. I smile wanly. My thoughts immediately turn to throwing up, not down, as I finish my second cup of coffee. My stomach hates me for it.

Ten minutes later, the Board of Directors spread out across the long table in the conference room. Their eyes drill me as I pitch our latest non-profit initiative to improve body image education in high schools. I appreciate the irony, but can't point this out to anyone else.

The coffee hits my stomach acid, hungry to consume and furious at being delivered only coffee yet again. My intestines growl. The board members hear it. They glance at each other and avoid looking at me in front of them, clutching my gut and grinning too widely. I speak over my stomach, but it's no use. You're hellbent on punishing me.

The black coffee snakes into my throat. It tastes like watery, infernal sludge. It burns like that too. I swallow it down. You will not win. I'm almost done. I can make it through this.

I feel my panties wet. Something trickles down the insides of my thighs, out of the hem of my dress, over my naked knees and squishes between my toes, exposed by a pair of peep toe pumps. A stream of brown urine stains my beige flesh, like the topography of a muddy river in a dry, dead land. *Not urine*, I think. But that isn't possible.

A wave of gasps sweeps the Board of Directors, twelve in total. I lose my breath. I want to give in. Run to you, crumble to my knees, throw my arms around you and nuzzle my face into your nook that fits my entire head like it was specially designed for me.

I clench a hand over my mouth. You can't make me come to you anymore.

Instead, there in the conference room, black coffee and bile spurt out of my mouth, sputter between my fingers and splatter across the grey and navy pebbled carpet. I double over and shake my head in shame. You won't stop there, though. This is retribution. You're a vengeful porcelain god full of wrath.

The audience groans. Behind my closed, humiliated eyes, board members hurl. An unsyncopated chorus of gagging and heaving. My director rushes out of the room. She has the self-control to wretch in a can out of view.

I collect my bag. My director meets me and daintily dabs a tissue at the corner of her mouth. She pats my shoulder.

"Go home. You're sick," she says.

I wonder what I've missed in all the time I've spent with you. I can't begin to calculate the minutes over the last decade. It's been more than a decade. I wasted childhood fantasies on you for years before I ever initiated our relationship.

What memories do I not hold dear because I was with you? What moments did I miss during family dinners before my grandmother died? What jokes do I not share, what pleasures might I have explored, what secrets, confessions and dreams might have been confided in me in all that missed time?

If I cannot end this once and for all, what will I lose with my daughter? Her first laugh, first steps, first words?

I won't let you steal anything more from me.

At home, my husband packs two overnight bags, one for him and one for our daughter. As he says goodbye for the night, he doesn't let me kiss our daughter's chubby cheeks. He holds her six feet away. I've blamed it on a stomach flu and she's not old enough for that vaccination.

"We can't take the risk that you might infect her," he says.

"You're right," I reply as I wave them goodbye. He doesn't know how right he is.

I stand on the porch long after the car turns the corner of our suburb into the sunset towards the nearest hotel. I return inside only when the spectrum of oranges and yellows receding into the horizon remind me of putrid stomach acid, bubbling and floating in toilet water. This is the first time I've been home alone in nearly a year. Since I found out I was pregnant. My husband is doting. He's practically welded himself to my hip. I love it because it steels me against you.

But here we are. Alone once again.

I open the fridge. I'm starving. I tell myself I won't overdo it. Just a bite. Not even a full meal. I scarf a Tupperware of leftovers down and wash it with a glass of water. Finished and sitting on the couch, I pretend that I'm not already thinking of you. I go back to the kitchen. Nibble a bag of popcorn. Start and finish a tube of my husband's favourite cookies. The remaining half of a pint of ice cream. Scramble and stuff my face with four eggs. Slowly but surely, I eat everything in sight until the kitchen is empty. If I could, I would eat the kitchen itself. Maybe then you would leave me alone.

I keel over and gasp for breath. My body can't handle this. Muscle memory kicks in. It's fighting to go back to our old ways. Look at that, you and I are 'we' and 'our' once again. How easily we slip back into old patterns.

I shake my head. I won't let it happen. I won't give into you.

I tear apart the junk drawer and find the sewing kit I've used once. My fingers shake as I aim the unbearably thin thread and miss the eye of the needle. It takes six tries to get it through. I remember how to properly knot it thanks to a home-ec class in high school. If only I knew then that the class's infantile lessons would be used for this purpose.

I use up three arm lengths of thread and proceed.

I dig the needle into the flesh of my bottom lip, up. I groan and fight against the pain. Blood sprinkles my hand and flows into the crevice of my working elbow, wet and sticky. I jab the needle through my thin upper lip. I plunge the needle half an inch over and back down through my bottom lip, back up my top lip, until my mouth is sewn shut.

It isn't enough.

I repeat this process three times, going back the other way, then back over twice more. When I tie the final knot and cut the needle off the dangling thread, I feel empowered. I march into the bathroom and stand akimbo above you. In the mirror is a shadow of the woman I should be. Slivers of fatty flesh protrude between imprecise stitches.

The string lifts the corners of my lips into a twisted smile, like a maniacal marionette.

I stand there, feet wide apart. Finally, I've conquered something. You didn't know the lengths I was capable of going. I didn't either. I guess you taught me some things about myself. I want to laugh. To say, "Look who's in control now." But I can't.

I realise too late my mistake.

The food bounds through me, twisting and turning up my organs. What can leak through the tight seams of my lips does. It's not enough. My mouth balloons from the pressure. My flesh rips. I won't let you win. I swallow it down, gulp by gulp.

It isn't enough. It comes back. I want to scream from the pain, but my voice traps there with a flood of puke that has nowhere to go. I'm fighting against my body now. I pry my fingers under the stitches, but they're so taut against my skin I can't find leverage. Vomit scented like battery acid waterfalls out my nose.

I'm drowning. Puke fills my lungs, an agonous fire.

I collapse against you, on my knees, arms sprawled around your curves. Your cold porcelain skin warms under my touch, as if you're welcoming me back with open arms. As if to say, you love me unconditionally, no matter how hard I try to turn my back on you. Mercy. I weep salty tears I can't taste. This is how my husband and daughter will find me. My secret exposed in this dying embrace.

Once upon a time, I thought I could never quit you. You were never going to let me.

EVELYN FREELING is a writer, mother, and wife from the Pacific Northwest. She grew up in what she still insists was a haunted house. She harbours an obsession for things that give her nightmares and for turning nightmares into stories.

FIRST HARVEST

April Yates

"I don't trust them," Freya said, her eyes tracking across the array of pots that littered the table. "Every time I look, they've shot up another inch."

"That's what plants do—they grow." Beth's thumb worked rapidly, spritzing the budding sprouts with an old-fashioned glass water mister. She looked the very picture of an Edwardian lady. Although in Freya's opinion it had to be the most inefficient means of water conveyance known to man; surely a watering can would be easier?

"I feel as if they've taken us over." The large patio doors faced east, so that was where Beth had dragged the Ping-Pong table so they could bathe in the morning sun. It was March, far too cold for them to go outside yet, so propagators, compostable pots, and trough planters were all filled with soon-to-be herbs and vegetables.

"Just think about when we have our first harvest. Imagine pizza made with our own tomatoes, garlic..." Beth sauntered over, planting a kiss on Freya's cheek. "Loads of fresh basil."

"You know I can't resist when you talk culinary."

“I promise, a few more weeks and they’ll all be outside.”

Freya awoke before Beth the next morning. As she drank her cup of tea, Freya examined the plants; it was the onions she found particularly insidious. The milky white tendrils breached through the confines of the compostable pots, searching, grasping for darkness. The sooner Beth planted them outside, the better.

“Hybrid seeds?” Freya at looked at the fine white flakes on Beth’s palm. “Hybrids of what exactly?”

Beth’s forehead crumpled in upon itself. Eventually, she answered.

“I’m not sure, some kind of orchid, rose combo.”

“Is that even possible?”

“I dunno.” Beth shrugged.

“I didn’t think you were interested in flowers. What happened to practicality? Being able to eat all you grow?” Freya gently teased.

“These are practical: the woman down at the allotments told me it will deter pests. It’s called companion planting.”

Even though Beth didn’t have an allotment—nor a reasonable chance of getting one, the waiting list being at least four years long—she’d started spending an inordinate amount of time there. Freya had teased that she must find wellington boots sexy. Beth had agreed and told Freya she should buy a pair.

Freya, for all of her teasing and moaning, was happy that Beth had found something to occupy her mind after three years of hormone injections, tracking temperatures and ovulation times. After three years of negative pregnancy tests.

Three years of crying on bathroom floors.

"Well, plant them. It'd be interesting to see if they turn out."

Weeks passed, with no sign that the hybrid seeds had taken. Most likely sterile, a quick Google search had told Beth. There was a slight grimace on her face as she relayed the information to Freya.

Certain words stung her, Freya knew. Words like "barren" and "sterile". After so long wrapping her identity around having a child, Beth had come to see these as a personal attack on her, no matter the context.

"Never mind." She closed the laptop abruptly.

"I'll ask that woman, when I next go down to the allotment."

"Who is this woman exactly? You've never told me her name."

Confusion fogged Beth's features.

"She must have told me, but I just can't remember." She shook her head, trying to dispel the mist. "It'll come back to me."

Beth came back from the allotment beaming the next day.

"What's got you in such a good mood?" Beth gave Freya a one-armed hug, her free hand clutching a brown paper envelope.

"I know what I've been doing wrong now, she explained it all to me."

Freya could only assume the "she" was Beth's new allotment friend.

"Excellent." Freya turned back to the sandwich she was halfway through making. "Do you want something to eat?"

She looked back up. Beth was gone, having slipped silently through the back door. Freya watched through the kitchen window as Beth made her way to the potting shed at the end of the garden, closing the door behind her so it sheltered her from view.

During the long Easter bank holiday, Beth spent sunrise to sunset away from Freya. On every one of those days, at one o'clock, Freya took a plate of food down to the shed where Beth had sequestered herself away. The door was locked the first two days; Beth opened the door when Freya knocked though, thanking her and taking the plate from her.

The third day, the Easter Sunday, she called out to just leave it.

On the fourth day, Beth had forgotten to lock the door. Freya stepped into the shed, expecting Beth to hurriedly push her out, so desperate had she been those last few days to hide.

Beth stood with her back to the door. She was hunched slightly forward, her arms straight to the bench, supporting her. Freya watched in rapt fascination as her shoulders contracted, relaxed, contracted, relaxed. The movement reminded Freya of a kitten kneading their mother whilst feeding.

She moved to her side, and saw that Beth had buried herself to her forearms in compost. Her eyes were closed; face bathed in the golden sunlight streaming from the narrow window. Never had she looked more terrifyingly beautiful than she did now.

Freya reached tentatively out, her fingertips lightly grazing Beth's cheek.

"Honey?"

Beth continued flexing her shoulders. Fine beads of sweat clung to her brow.

"Honey," Freya said, louder this time, yet Beth still didn't respond.

"Beth!" Freya grasped Beth's shoulder, giving it a gentle shake. Beth opened her eyes.

"What are you doing?"

"Oh, I was…" Beth's eyes darted around the shed, looking at anything but Freya.

"I was mixing plant food pellets in with the compost. It's very therapeutic. I must've drifted off."

Beth's hands remained buried in the compost.

"Are you done?"

Freya pointed at the pot. Beth looked down, then up again.

"Yes," she said, making no move to disinter herself.

"I'm worried about you."

Beth responded to Freya's words with an icy stare. Diamond hard eyes fixed on her.

"Why? This is what you've always wanted, isn't it? Me, distracted from all the baby talk? I think you were secretly glad when we stopped trying, but you're too much of a coward to come out and say it."

Freya stood dumbstruck. She opened her mouth to protest, but quickly closed it again. Beth continued to stare.

"So don't you worry. I'm fine. I'm always fine," Beth said, through clenched teeth, hands still buried, but balled tight; Freya could tell from the tension in her arms.

She knew Beth was far from fine, but Freya was far too pissed off now to engage further. Unwilling to risk thorny words, she stomped back to the house, slamming the door behind her.

Trying to shut out the thought that maybe she was a coward.

"I'm sorry," Beth whispered in the dark as she climbed into bed next to Freya. ''You know the last thing I'd ever want to do is frighten or worry you."

The air was redolent with a sweet, heady, unfamiliar perfume; Freya briefly wondered when Beth had bought it, but soon her senses were reeling from it and the thought was buried deep.

Beth ran her fingers under the cover, along Freya's bare thigh. She shivered in response to Beth's touch.

But something was wrong, something that tinged the normal shiver of excitement with slight revulsion. Beth's fingers felt strange, as if covered in soft notches.

As Beth carried on with her ministrations, Freya's resolve gave way; she sought Beth's mouth, her search rewarded with a kiss tasting of raspberries and rhubarb.

Freya felt utterly intoxicated, head swimming as she reached out, but this time Beth remained elusive.

“No, I want tonight to be all about you. I’m going to take care of you.”

The holiday was over, and it was time to go back to work. Freya would normally lament the end of time spent at home alone with Beth. This time, however, she welcomed it.

Despite the lovemaking the night before, there was still something off about Beth. It hadn’t felt like it at the time, but Beth must have been rough.

Spots of blood had stained the bedsheet and a dull ache resided deep in Freya’s abdomen.

Freya was sure going back to work would kick start normality and Beth’s new obsession would be tempered. But when Beth appeared at the breakfast table wearing gardening gloves, it drove a bolt of despair into Freya’s chest.

They sat in silence, Beth slowly sipping at a glass of water, having refused food and her usual morning cup of tea.

Freya got up from the table.

“I’ll leave you to clear up, seeing as how you’ve decided to stay home.”

The house was exactly as Freya left it when she returned eight hours later. She walked through the kitchen, past the dishes, and out the back door.

Beth was dozing on a sun lounger on the patio, naked, yet still wearing her gardening gloves.

Freya knelt beside her. She placed her palm on Beth's stomach; she didn't stir. Beth was hot to the touch—not surprising—but the texture of her skin was soft velvet.

Like a flower petal.

Beth slept while Freya sat at the kitchen table, watching the sky turn from azure to amethyst before settling on jet.

When Beth finally shuffled through the door, she went straight to the sink. Turning it on, she pressed her lips to the stream of water, drinking deeply. Thirst quenched, she moved—still in that trance-like state—to the door, making her way upstairs. Still nude, save for those fucking gloves.

Freya followed, Beth oblivious to her pleas to stop and just talk to her. Desperate, she grabbed at Beth's hand. The glove shed like snakeskin.

Freya screamed.

Beth's hand—the hand that Freya had held through all the doctor's appointments, the hand that had touched and caressed her so many times—was now a mass of white tendrils writhing. Without the glove, they quickly lost their shape. Freya clutched the glove; it was damp and filled with compost—a portable pot.

"You need help," Freya whispered. "Whatever's happening to you, we can fix it together. I love you."

"This isn't something that needs fixing. You're going to see that soon."

Beth took the glove back. Freya watched in a horror as the tendrils rearranged themselves to fit, pulling the glove back on without aid.

"I'm going to call someone." Freya reached into her pocket for her mobile. "I should have done this when I got home."

"I said no!" Beth swatted at the phone, sending it clattering across the floor.

"Really?" Freya said, as she bent to retrieve it. She felt a sharp pain in her shoulder before being yanked away from the phone.

"I can't let you do that."

Beth held Freya fast.

"You're hurting me."

Beth relaxed her grip on Freya, who gave a sigh of relief. *I'm getting through to her*, she thought. Beth still held her, but it was no longer painful.

"Thank you. Let's talk…"

Freya felt a sharp barb pierce her neck. The colours of the world bled together into an iridescent oil slick, then all went black.

The sun streamed through the bedroom window. Freya tried to turn away from the light, but a heavy numbness pervaded her body from the neck down. At the very corner of her peripheral vision, Freya could see Beth siting in shadow.

"Beth." Tears filled Freya's eyes. "What have you done?"

"This is for us." Beth's voice sounded thin. Reedy. "I can't believe how quickly it all happened, though. I thought I'd have to keep you under another week."

"Another week?" Freya repeated. "You've kept me here, unconscious, for a week?"

"Six days, to be precise. I can feel the time is near and I couldn't let you miss it. You might not understand yet, but one day you'll thank me. That we were all together for the moment."

Freya shifted slightly, the effects of the paralysis beginning to wear off. Using her elbows, she lifted herself to a siting position.

Beth was still bathed in shadow, but from her new vantage point Freya could make out strange new facets of her silhouette. Protrusions unnatural crowned her head. Freya had always called Beth her Queen. What a cruel cosmic joke this was.

"Do you know, they are still discovering new species of orchids in South America? All kinds of plant life we know nothing-to-little about." She gave a choked chuckle. "You can be the one to claim discovery of me, Freya."

Beth rose from the chair and moved to stand in the window, the sun blazing behind her.

She was no longer one, but a multitude.

Petals adorned her, a coat of ruffled scales, her new colours gold and purple.

Regal. Freya wondered if Beth'd had influence over her new form.

Pods hung like overripe fruit from her abdomen, spring green and ridged.

One pulsated in sympathy with Freya's own heartbeat.

"I'm not barren anymore," Beth said, stretching out her arms, the tangles of which had thickened and twisted together to form a hand that gleamed a healthy white.

"I've been transformed into the most fertile being that's ever been. With your help, of course. I had to take something from you, but it's nothing we hadn't already discussed doing. It's better this way. This way, it's fully a part of both of us."

She sat on the bed beside Freya, one appendage stroking Freya's thigh. The other unbuttoned the pyjama top she wore, pushing it open in a cruel parody of the nights they had spent in this bed.

"Please don't." The words came out choked, her tears flowing fast now.

Beth withdrew. "You always said I was talented with my hands, Freya. I reckon I could do so much better with these. When you're ready, of course."

Freya couldn't tear her eyes away from Beth's abdomen, the way she stroked the quivering pod absently as she continued to speak.

"It's beautiful, isn't it? Being able to take a part of you into me, to grow and nurture. All the time and money we spent. All those doctors with their science. I should have trusted in Mother Nature all along. If only I'd known how quick and simple it could have been. You know, I think that's why you lost interest towards the end. You had too much time to think about it all. You got scared."

The pod's movement quickened. Beth stood back up.

"It's time."

Her faux fingers wrapped around the pod, twisting it slightly as she pulled it away from her body.

The pod unfurled, revealing a squirming mass of roots. At its centre, a tiny human heart fluttered. Freya watched as the white filament knitted and knotted together to form a vaguely humanoid shape.

Beth placed it on Freya's bare chest, its handlike tendrils pawing and grasping at her hair.

Its heartbeat slowed as it settled between her breasts, content with the reunion.

"Isn't it wonderful, darling?" Beth sighed. "Our first harvest."

APRIL YATES lives in Derbyshire with her wife and two fluffy demons masquerading as dogs. She should be working on her novella about the horrors of Golden Age Hollywood, but is easily distracted by the squirrels in her garden. Find her on Twitter @April_Yates_ and tell her to get back to work, or aprilyates.com.

TOO HEAVY TO CARRY

Faye Snowden

This was Ojah's habit, to stand at the iron gate as many times as she could, hoping that one day her run-off daddy would saunter down that road and back home to her. Today might be her one lucky day. A dark spot no bigger than the pad of her thumb hung there in the shimmering heat, becoming larger the longer Ojah stared. She thought this was the day that something would come from all the hoping and waiting.

But it wasn't her father whistling like a songbird coming down that road.

It was a woman with hips that swayed easily beneath a full skirt. She made her way toward Ojah, full of confidence about where she had been and where she needed to be. *She walks*, Ojah thought, *as if she's been called.*

She stopped abruptly in front of Ojah, her skirts swaying with remembered movement. Ojah's eyes travelled up from the woman's broad skirts, to her thick waist and over her ample bosom, moving until they reached the woman's headwrap. Shades of black and the darkest blues roiled in the thick cloth. Ojah imagined that the woman had snatched down the scariest, darkest sky she could find and swirled it witch-like about her head. Ojah rubbed her eyes. The headwrap became just another piece of clothing that many slave women wore. Nothing special about it.

The woman bent down until her face was level with Ojah's. She had a face that gave nothing away—not her age, who her people were, or what kind of thoughts roamed behind her pure black eyes. It was broad and flat, like a plank. For a moment, Ojah thought that God had forgotten to put his mark on her.

"What do they need?" the woman asked, pointing to the plantation house sequestered in the shade of willows and twisting oak. Ojah grew up in that house upon the orders of the mistress, Rowena Holton. Rowena wanted to raise a girl slave child inside the plantation house. She wanted someone loyal, someone reared straight from the womb whose only mission was to serve her. But nowadays, Rowena would say every time she saw Ojah, "Lord, but who knew you would be so black!"

Four loud finger snaps in Ojah's face. Ojah blinked.

"What do they need?" the woman repeated, impatient.

"You mean them in the house?" Ojah said. "I don't know."

The woman showed her one long index finger, the nail sharp like a knife. "You know exactly. Not knowing would get you killed. What's your name?"

"Lilbit." It was by instinct that Ojah spoke the name that Rowena had given her at birth.

“I’m not talking about your slave name. What is your cabin name? What do your people call you when your master and mistress are not around?”

“Ojah. My daddy called me Ojah.”

Grey and black shadows moved in the headwrap as the woman stood up. Ojah took a step back.

“Everybody need something, Ojah,” she said. She pointed back to the house. “What do *they* need?”

“A cook,” Ojah said. “They ain’t got a cook.”

“What happened to the one they had?”

“She got burnt.”

“How?”

“Too many bad pies. Gravy always lumpy. Mistress said the cook did it on purpose to shame her before folk.”

The woman waited.

“The cook was frying chicken. Grease hot,” Ojah said. “Got burned. Seem like her eye melted right out of her face.”

“Where is she now? The old cook.”

Ojah waved a small hand toward the cotton fields. “Mistress say she too ugly to work in the house.”

Rowena sent Ojah to live in the quarters with Ojah’s brother Jiles several months after the new cook hired herself out to the Holtons. Ojah took to the way Jiles held her face between his big hands; the warm note in his voice when he called her sister. She felt finally home. Jiles’ best friend Apollo treated her like blood, too. Having them both around made her feel almost as safe as she felt when her daddy was around.

One night as she and Jiles readied for bed, Ojah asked of the raised scars on Jiles' back, "Did it hurt?"

He laughed. "Did it hurt? Yeah, it hurt. Tealow ain't no joke with the lash."

He turned to face her once they settled on their pallets, while the candle's flame whispered in the darkness.

"You remember seeing our daddy get whipped, Ojah?"

She considered. She remembered standing in the doorway of the kitchen house, watching. Jiles was there, too, but on the opposite side of the yard in a group of field slaves that Holton forced to watch. Tealow, the overseer, didn't do the whipping that time. It was Holton himself.

The whip flew high each time he raised his arm, the lash growing thinner and thinner with every inch of bright blue sky it gained. It whistled a terrible song on the way down to her daddy's back, the flesh splitting open with each touch. Her daddy answered with a curdling scream.

He survived the beating, and when he became strong enough, he ran. Tealow and Holton went after him, but returned with nothing. It was then that Ojah took up her vigil by the gate to watch the dusty road for any sign of his return, never mind that the old folk kept telling her that if he did return, it would be as a ghost.

"I'll tell you what," Jiles said. "Ain't nobody gonna whip me like they whipped Daddy. I swear to God up in his heaven, and if he ain't listening, then I swear to the devil. Ain't nobody."

Barbary, the new cook, came down to the slave quarters the following Sunday. The slaves murmured 'hellos' and 'how yous' as she passed. She answered, but didn't look at them. Her eyes were fixed on Ojah, who stood in the doorway of the cabin she shared with Jiles. Barbary stopped in front of Ojah, but didn't say anything. Finally, Ojah spoke, "The old cook slept in the kitchen house."

Barbary shifted the bundle on her head. "I'm not the old cook. I like being in the quarter with my folk."

Barbary removed the bundle and set it on the ground. She took out a few clothes and other things to get at the cold chicken wings, stale biscuits and a few shrivelled potatoes wrapped in muslin like Christmas gifts. She passed the extra food out to the slaves who had gathered around.

When they left, Barbary said, "I hope that's all right with you? That you can spare some room in your cabin."

Ojah, and later Jiles said she could, and that was that. Barbary helped her clear a patch for a fall garden, taught Ojah how to weed and how to plant, all the while telling stories of her adventures far away as they dropped the seeds into the rich soil.

Ojah worked in the fields every day except Sundays. Tealow made her help the old one-eyed cook pass out water to the pickers, and run errands. Ojah watched Jiles glide up and down the rows, the bags hanging fat as soon as he started and growing fatter as he went. His fingers flew between the cotton stalks like the wings of a hummingbird. One day, he winked at her as he passed, a triumphant smile on his lips.

"Ain't nothing to be smiling at, gal," the old cook said. "That boy must be praying for the Devil to open the door to hell. He courting trouble."

"He's doing good. Look how much he picked," Ojah said. "He's finally beating Apollo."

"What happens when he don't pick so good tomorrow?"

Tealow weighed Jiles' bag when the day had cooled and the last of the sun shone through a haze of red. Everybody was usually quiet during the weighing, but today the silence made Ojah's heart beat faster.

"Almost 200 pounds. You been holding out on me, boy. Bring me 220 tomorrow." Tealow stopped talking, eyed the men and women gathering around the scales. "And I expect all the rest of you boys to bring me in what this boy done brung today. You gals add another twenty pounds to your normal haul."

Later that night, Jiles stumbled into the cabin, groaning as he removed his shirt and laid down on the straw mat next to Ojah. Barbary rose and lit the candle to reveal a bruised face, Jiles' left eye bulging and turning black.

"What happened?" Barbary asked.

"Got beat up. Both me and Apollo. Everybody said it's our fault that they got to pick more tomorrow."

"But Tealow won't be expecting that now, right? You sick," Ojah said.

The flickering candle was the loudest thing in the room. Finally, he said, "They don't care how sick a body is. They say pick. You pick."

"What you gonna do?" Ojah asked.

"I don't know."

When they all lined up to work the next morning, both Jiles and Apollo were missing.

Ojah was at the gate the following Sunday when they brought Jiles back. Holton came first on a big black horse, and then Tealow on an old mare dragging Jiles' uncovered body on a sled made from sticks. Ojah ran ahead of the horses to the quarter to find Barbary.

Holton jumped down from his horse just as Ojah emerged from the cabin holding Barbary's hand. He snatched the hat from his head and threw it on the ground. "Running away." He looked at them in turn. Heads dropped as his gaze fell on them. "Just where in Jesus you think you running to? You think you gonna get through these woods to the border so you'd be free? Not as long as I have breath in my body."

No one said anything. Not a murmur. Even the quarter dogs who usually yipped and yapped at every little thing deferred to the deep quiet rumbling among the slaves. The dogs sniffed the air around the body. They waited.

“The only freedom you gone get will be in the bye-and-bye, and that ain’t no guarantee.” Holton threw a careless gesture toward the travois.

“Tealow,” he said. “Get that boy off of there.”

Tealow untied the travois from the mare. The quiet turned different when Jiles’ body fell all the way to the ground with a wet thump. It was no longer about not talking. It was about not thinking. About pushing the hurt so far down into your body that even your soul can’t find it.

Only the old one-eyed cook spoke. She said, “Oh, lord have mercy!”

He had been in the water. The river that the old folk complained was not water at all, but something living and mean, something with hands that snatched slave children who got too close, pulled them down to the place they called the gone-forever.

Holton said, “Next time when you have a beating coming to you, just take it.” He picked up his hat and swung away toward the plantation house.

“What happened to my boy, massa?” a woman said to Holton’s retreating back. “Apollo.”

“Tealow,” Holton said without turning around.

Everyone had been so busy watching Jiles that the lump on the back of the mare escaped attention. Tealow removed the blanket from Apollo’s body, untied him from the mare. Tealow gave the body the slightest shove. It rolled off the mare and fell to the ground by Jiles. Where Apollo's stomach should have been was a bloody hole. His mama wailed.

"Gut shot," Tealow said. "He ran. Took us some time to catch up to him. The animals got to him first. Ate the soft parts. Dragged his guts all over them woods."

Tealow had refused to let them move the bodies. That night with Jiles and Apollo laying in the cabin's front yard, Barbary tossed and mumbled in her sleep about long bloody ropes. She lay on the pallet next to Ojah, sweating and low-talking. The next day, Barbary walked around the dead boys, fingers moving over the collar of her dress in rhythm with her constant mutterings. She told Ojah that if the demons that had hold of her didn't let go soon, she would have to go out there and lay beside Jiles and Apollo.

Rowena came down to the cabin the next morning. Barbary had been well enough to stand, and was able to make it to the door when Rowena hollered for her to come outside.

"I cannot afford another lazy cook," Rowena said, a cloth soaked in rosewater pressed to her face. "My birthday dinner is in four days. I've invited my entire family. You should be cooking by now."

"I've been sick, Mistress," Barbary said.

Rowena shot a glance at the rotting bodies in front of the cabin. "I'll have Tealow clean that up. Maybe that would keep you from playing sick."

"I haven't been playing."

“Really? You look plenty fine to me.”

“I ain’t been fine. My guts twisting all the time. I can’t keep nothing down. And my eyes bothering me something fierce.”

She was telling the truth because Ojah had been a witness. Everything the cook ate, no matter how small, came back up in a thick mud tinged with red reminiscent of blood. Barbary saw things all the time, complained like someone seeing to the other side of the grave. Ojah heard her talking to the old folks about silver wings fluttering around her eyes. She begged them to pick out the eggs the flies laid on the surface of her eyeballs.

“You don’t think I know how y’all are? Playing sick so you don’t have to work? Pretending like you forget and burning my pies? I know you people, especially you women. You tell your body to do all sorts of things, and your body just does it, your flesh minding your nasty thoughts like it’s some sort of religion.”

“That’s not right,” Barbary said.

Rowena ignored her.

“If your lazy ass ain’t in the kitchen house tonight, it won’t be your entrails that I hang from the pot racks, it will be the severed black head of this gal you’ve grown so fond of. Lord knows you had better quarters in the kitchen house. I will not be shamed before my family, not again. I will have this dinner party, and you will cook.”

Barbary looked down at Ojah, and Ojah stared back up, trying to read her face.

“Ain’t no need to hurt this chile,” Barbary finally said. “I’ll do like you say.”

On the night of the birthday dinner Rowena Holton didn't look like a woman who days earlier threatened to behead an eight-year-old. The pale pink gown she wore left her scented shoulders bare. A blood red rose crafted from delicate silk nestled between her breasts, while dozens of them ringed the bottom of her overskirt. She flitted from guest to guest, laughing and talking, telling them what dishes to try, how they came by the menu, how glad she was that they took time to visit on her birthday. The dozen or so guests were all Rowena's family—her in-laws, her sister, and several cousins to whom she loved playing the grand lady.

Ojah herself wore a dress with a red velvet bodice to match the velvet of the two slave boys working the punkahs. Rowena ordered them under the threat of death not to stop fanning until the last guest had left the house. There would be no flies buzzing among the candlelight glimmering in the silver candelabras, or hovering over the stuffed goose on the sparkling porcelain plates. Ojah and the rest of the slaves hustled, running dish after dish to the table, refilling the crystal goblets with red wine or water when requested. She whisked away empty plates amid the happy noise. Ojah was young for this work, but trained to it from the time she could walk. If she did a good job, maybe the Holtons would leave Barbary alone for a while. Let her rest.

The only problem was Barbary herself. She kept coming from the kitchen-house into the dining room, which was something that the old cook never did. Ojah suspected that one of the reasons Rowena kept jumping up from the table was to hide the cook and the cook's confused mutterings, the big hands batting the air in front of her face. Ojah wondered how no one else noticed the colours in the headwrap becoming richer as the night continued on. Black giving way to hues of dark blues, before returning to the colour of midnight.

Later, when wine and good food had sweetened the conversation and increased the frequency of laughter, Ojah thought that everything would be all right. Rowena was sitting down for once. Plates of puddings and glazed lemon cake passed from hand to hand while Ojah filled the delicate coffee cups.

Barbary remained in the dining room. She stood watching the gaily dressed men and women at the dining room table. Rowena sent Barbary several looks sharp enough to cut, but the cook didn't notice or care. One moment her hands would be calmly folded in front of her, the next they'd jerk in front of her face or rub her eyes as if they were filled with grit. A time or two, Barbary mumbled, causing several guests to turn her way.

"Your cook, my dear," one of the cousins, Roscoe, said. He stroked the embroidered purple wildflowers on the high silk collar of his waistcoat and continued, "seems to suffer from dysaesthesia aethiopica. I read about it in De Bow's."

"I beg your pardon?" Rowena said.

"A mental disease," Roscoe said. "Particular to the African. Maybe your husband has heard of it?"

"I have," Holton grunted. "But I don't believe it. Just pure laziness."

"Not at all, dear cousin. It's a disease. Makes it hard for them to feel things, even pain. I'm afraid this insensibility to touch also affects the mind. Makes them walk about at night, sleep during the day. See things. Become touched in the head like your cook. I hear it's worse in females."

"Though the food is quite delicious," Rowena said cheerfully. Everyone laughed. "How is your cake, Roscoe? Cook made it special for my birthday."

"Nonsense," Holton said. "Some slaves just need a good taste of the whip."

"Let's not talk about it," Rowena said. "We've had a wonderful evening. And besides, she's working now."

"But will she be tomorrow? I bet she takes to bed for days. Look at her," Roscoe said.

And they did. All of them. Bright heads turning to Barbary, who was again batting the air in front of her face.

"Goes along with drapetomania as well," Roscoe said. He took a bite of cake, chewed and thought, said nothing more.

"Are you going to enlighten us as to what you mean?" Holton said.

"It's a disease that enchants the African into running away. You did have that happen several times, an incident quite recently, I believe."

"I do not like this kind of talk," Rowena said. "It's unpleasant. And why is the soup still on the table in the middle of desert? Lilbit!"

The cousin and Holton continued sparing as Ojah walked to the table to take the soup tureen, a dish she knew to be heavy and awkward.

"Two slaves ran away," Holton said. "And it wasn't from any disease. They wanted to keep from getting the beating they deserved."

"But that was a large loss to you, right?"

"Four or five thousand dollars, yes. Though I believe it is coarse to bring up money at my dear wife's birthday dinner."

"A lot of money," Roscoe continued, taking another bite of the sweet cake.

Holton laughed. "Maybe for you. But not for me. Besides, I don't keep freedom-thinking slaves around. Spoils the others."

"But you do go after them," Roscoe said. "To sell them, because you need the money."

Holton stopped, looked around at his dinner guests. He took a deep drink of his whiskey before sitting back in his chair.

"Let me tell you a story," Holton said. "I had another run not too long before those two boys did. I took care of it, but didn't bother bringing back his body. Let the animals deal with it. They didn't believe me down in the quarter, that he was gone. Thought if they couldn't see his rotting flesh, he had to be alive."

Holton sat the now empty whiskey glass on the table, his face pink with drink, his eyes glassy. He said, "Slaves need to see the example, need to smell what will happen to them if they run. That's why I brought back them other boys, Jiles and Apollo."

"Robert," Rowena exclaimed. "Please. We are at dinner!"

"So those in the quarter can see that if you run, you die," Holton rambled on. "Just like the idiot before Jiles and Apollo. Why, I blew that fool's head off while he begged for his life, talking about don't I care about Lilbit. Had Tealow throw that worthless piece of meat in the river. I bet the quarter won't say he ran away, now. Not after getting a look at the bodies I just brought back."

Ojah dropped the tureen. The heavy porcelain crashed to the floor, sending streams of turtle soup into the air, splashing full onto Rowena's gown.

Rowena gasped. Her chest heaved as she stood up. She shook out the skirt of her gown and turned to her guests. The crash had silenced the room. Even the punkah stopped.

"You see what she has done?" Rowena said.

Ojah crept backward as softly as she could. Her father had been dead all along, she thought. All this time.

"You," Rowena pointed at her. "You don't move an inch."

Petticoats swinging, she moved toward Ojah. She raised her hand. Ojah shut her eyes tight, her entire body cringed in anticipation of the blow, waiting for physical pain to be added to her grief.

But none came. She opened her eyes to see Barbary's broad back, the black headwrap on her stately head.

"No," Barbary said.

Ojah came around just in time to see Holton stand up. Barbary pushed Ojah aside and walked to meet the man.

Suddenly, Holton stopped and twirled, slowly at first, as if he were about to start a difficult dance. He then twirled faster and faster, arms flailing, a look of surprise on his face.

"Why, he's having a fit," Roscoe said.

"No, it's her," Rowena said, pointing at Barbary.

"Witch!" another woman said.

Roscoe drew a small revolver from his coat and pointed it at Barbary.

"Stop," he said, his voice calm, as if he were already rehearsing in his head how he would tell the story later.

Barbary sent a look Roscoe's way, no more than a glance. His eyes bugged, and his mouth fell open. He turned the weapon toward himself. He opened his mouth and placed the gun there, pulled the trigger, sending a spray of blood, bone, and brain onto the silk wallpaper.

More men drew their weapons, and the room became misty with their blood. A few others rushed toward Barbary, but barely reached her before their bodies were flung backwards to smack the opposite wall. They slid down in a jumble of broken bones and loose flesh. Those who tried to flee fared no better. Barbary simply broke their necks. She did so without raising a hand in the effort.

Barbary turned back to Holton.

A great ripping sound filled the room as his clothes peeled from his body. His first moments of surprise when the twirling started gave way to what Ojah thought of as soul-screaming. The air around him began to hum a fast and terrible tune that ended with a loud snap. The naked flesh on Holton's back flayed open, exposing fat and then muscle and then bone.

He fell to the floor, trying to make his body small enough that the whip wouldn't find it. But the invisible whip kept coming, each whistle culminating into a loud snap. Holton tried to stand, but something pinned him. He begged. He begged for his wife, who stood looking at him with her mouth open, not moving, too horrified to run. When he saw she wasn't coming, he begged God, then the Devil, and finally Barbary, who just stood there pinning him with her gaze.

He flipped over onto his ripped back like a fish, his fat belly straining in order to keep his back from touching the floor. That was when the flies, as large and as black as crows, came. They stopped above Holton's straining belly and waited, their silvery wings flapping. A moment later, his stomach burst open. Intestines ascended from his gut and twirled around each other in a long, twisted rope. The flies attacked, sliding down the rope into the cavity that was once Holton's stomach. They crawled from the cavity onto his naked chest, buzzed around his eyes. Not until Holton's head was encased in the fat black bodies did Barbary turn to Rowena.

Rowena's screams filled the dining room. She ran but tripped over Roscoe, her foot becoming so tangled in Roscoe's destroyed mouth that she had to kick several times to free herself. She whipped up and ran for the door, but there was Barbary blocking Rowena's path to freedom. Rowena walked backward, put her hands out in front of her, pleading with Barbary to stay back.

Shadows lashed out from the headwrap. Fingers of smoke took a hold of Rowena's face. She screeched and fell to her knees. The smell of hot grease and burning flesh licked the polish from the shiny floors, the dust from the corners of the room. The flesh on the left side of Rowena's face melted from the bone, exposing every inch of her back teeth. The ringlets she had so patiently curled in anticipation of the biggest night of the year, her birthday, were on fire. She could feel everything. Ojah was sure of that. Rowena tried to talk, but could only gurgle in a rhythm that sounded like more begging.

But Barbary didn't stop. She just stared as a single drop of blood purled on Rowena's soft throat. The drop then moved, very slowly, leaving in its wake a steady line of garnet, which eventually grew wider and wider until blood spurted from her yawning neck. The screaming stopped.

The severed head hit first. Then the body, which was soon joined by a contingent of the feasting flies.

Ojah and Barbary were the only two living souls left in the room. Ojah was covered in blood. Barbary was covered in blood. Ojah looked at Barbary. Barbary looked at Ojah. The headwrap had regained its original colour, which now looked positively dull compared to how it had been during dinner.

Barbary said, "Sorry you had to see that, Chile."

She reached under the headwrap and took out two small glass vials. She walked over to Rowena and slid Rowena's blood into one of the vials. She capped it. She then walked over to Holton. She kneeled over his opened belly. The flies rose up immediately, undulating in black waves as Barbary filled the second vial.

"Sometimes the pain just gets too heavy to carry," Barbary said, twisting the second vial tight. "And I just have to put it back where it belongs."

When Ojah returned to the quarters, the slaves were already packing up, throwing everything they could get their hands on into Holton's carriages and wagons. The old one-eyed cook sat atop her big black horse, cackling. Ojah returned to the front gate while they were packing in time to see Barbary walking down the same road she had come in on, her gait slow and steady, her stately shoulders set in a simmering calm, the headwrap that had once burned so brightly now one with a moonless night.

FAYE SNOWDEN writes noir mysteries, poems and short stories from her home in Northern California. Her short story, "One. Bullet. One Vote" was selected as one of the best American mystery and suspense stories of 2021. Novels include the Louisiana Killing *series featuring homicide detective Raven Burns.* A Killing Rain *will be out in 2022. Learn more about Faye at fayesnowden.com.*

FACES OF SETH

Vivian Kasley

I was fourteen and in eighth grade. I don't recall knowing Mr Peyton's age, but he had a wife and a baby, so I assumed he was at least in his early thirties. He knew how old I was; he drove our school bus. I sat in the front, my legs crossed, head down, usually in a book. If I happened to look up, he'd smile and catch my eye in the mirror. He was always watching from behind his sunglasses, always staring.

One Thursday, as I was stepping off the bus, he asked me if I could babysit for him and his wife the following weekend. I'd paused with my backpack on one shoulder and chewed my bottom lip to bide time. My gut was practically screaming at me to say no, but I ignored its pleas and said yes. Why wouldn't I have? Why shouldn't I have trusted the man who our parents and school trusted enough to drive us back and forth five days a week? And now, his face is burned into my silver-grey eyes, a horrific after image that never fades.

Mr Peyton answered the door in a ripped tee shirt and jeans. His shaggy sandy hair hung over one eye, and he flopped it over by blowing air up at it from his mouth. I greeted him and he immediately told me to please call him Seth, saying that Mr Peyton was way too formal and made him sound old. The sour tang of unwashed sweat and beer wafted from him when he reached out and ushered me inside as if he was hiding me from an unseen assailant. He shut the door, then grinned and said my hair reminded him of spun honey. I thanked him, then looked around and swallowed the dry lump that had formed in my throat. It became very evident that the house had been emptied of his wife and child.

My face felt flushed, and my pulse beat like a drum in my ears. I'd begun to feel the same way I had when I'd went sailing once—woozy and unsteady—and asked where the bathroom was. I sat down on the toilet and thought about what excuse I'd give my mother—who was so proud of me for taking my first paying babysitting job—if I called her to come and get me only minutes after she'd dropped me off.

When I came out of the bathroom, he was waiting by the door. He was tapping his nicotine-stained fingernails against the wall, his dark eyes studying my face. He asked me if I was alright, and I nodded. I asked him where everyone was. He said Mrs Peyton had forgotten that she and their son were supposed to go to her sister's house for the weekend and had cancelled their dinner date. He said not to worry, that he'd still pay me for my trouble and that we shouldn't waste a perfectly good Saturday evening just because his wife was a Silly Sally. Panic zapped my innards like a horde of electric eels, but still, I stayed.

He ordered a pepperoni pizza, and then we sat on the couch and ate and drank Rolling Rocks while discussing our favourite movies and music. He laughed when a gob of cheese and pepperoni from my slice of pizza dropped onto my shirt and then asked me if I wanted to take my shirt off and wear one of his. I'd shaken my head and murmured no thank you and he had shrugged and said suit yourself. When he started to slur his words, I stood up and said that I should call my mother to come and get me, but he grabbed my hand and pulled me back down onto the couch. His rank breath was hot in my ear and then on my neck as he whispered my name over and over, "Holly, Holly, Holly." The sound of my name coming from his mouth reminded me of someone panting. Then I let him touch my knee, and then he touched my thigh, and then and then and then…

I cried and laid as stiff as a corpse afterward. His nails tap, tap, tapped against the glass coffee table like drops of fat rain. He smoked a cigarette and then lit a joint, chuckling as he blew the skunky-smelling smoke toward my face. He choked and coughed until I thought he'd keel over, then growled at me to get the fuck up and wash my hairy cunt. Though I was afraid to move, I did as he told me. He followed me into the bathroom and watched as I washed; his face a distorted demon looming through the frosted shower doors.

Under the scalding water, my pale skin turned pink, but I still couldn't stop shivering. I cried and rubbed a bar of Irish Spring over the gross feeling that clung to me like an invisible fungus. When I got out, he wrapped me in a towel, patted my head like a dog, and told me to put my clothes back on. There was money sticking out of one of the pockets in my shorts, so I put my hand in and pulled free two crisp twenty-dollar bills. For your services, he'd said, grinning from ear to ear.

In his car, he gripped the steering wheel with one hand and stroked my leg with the other. He told me not to tell anyone, that we'd both get into big trouble. I stared out the window through watery eyes and said nothing. Before I could flee from the vehicle, he yanked me back by my hair hard enough to cause me to cry out. "If you tell anyone about this," he said, baring his teeth, "I promise you'll regret it." Then his face changed, and he smiled a sinister smile and chirped, "Hey now, cheer up, buttercup. I'll see you on Monday, bright and early, little girlie."

After that night, I was no longer me. I was someone else. Someone sullied and ruined. The bottled secret became like a slow drip of poison, weakening me and breaking me down. My decaying heart pumped my toxic blood through my veins and supplied my withering body with enough of its poison to keep me somewhat functional. Believe me, I tried to end it, but I was always brought back, stuffed full of pills, and then forced to face strangers who feigned empathy for the pretty sullen girl, the teenage freak who was sad for no good reason. *Cheer up, buttercup!*

Years passed, but my emotional growth had been stunted and my cells remained frozen in that one moment in time. They had failed to renew and regenerate a better me, or even fade some of the rottenest parts. They'd been too damaged by their putrid environment and had instead mutated, not into a cancer, but into something else, something that resembled exactly what I felt like. Once I'd accepted and embraced it, an electrical current ran through my body and re-awakened me. I'd risen from the dead and was alive again. I was unleashed and needed nourishment.

I am eighteen. Seth's face looms in front of me, and when he leans in to kiss me and whispers my name, I slash his throat and stab him, over and over, until he falls backward, convulses, and stops moving. My blade—which is shaped like the claw of a beast—is sharp and I straddle him, and carve an H into his face, leaving my mark. When I stand back up, it's no longer Seth's face. It has faded in death like a werewolf who's been shot with a silver bullet. It is only when I am gone that I realise what I've done.

I am twenty-five. Seth's face looms in front of me, and when he slides his hand up my thigh and leans in to kiss me and whispers my name, I pierce his chest, and I stab him, over and over, until he chokes on his blood and nothing but red foam bubbles from his twisted mouth. My blade is still sharp, and I carve an H into his face, leaving my mark. Again, it turns out not to be you, Seth. I know what I've done and do not care.

I am thirty-two. Seth's face looms in front of me, and when he sets his wine glass down and leans in to kiss me and whispers my name, I scream and I stab him, over and over, until he weeps for his mother the way I did for mine that night. My blade is sharper than ever and I carve an H into his face, leaving my mark. It's still not you, but I already know I'll do it again.

I am forty-five. Seth's face looms in front of me, again, as it always has, and when he leans in to kiss me and whispers my name, I stab, over and over, until he looks back at me with confusion and fear, and then with nothing at all. I use my blade—slightly duller now, but still sharp—to carve an H into his face, leaving my mark. It will always be Seth, until I feel I've severed the thick tether of shame that keeps me bound to him. I will always be the monster that he helped to create. A monster whose skin fits me now like a well-tailored suit. I've become comfortable in this skin and have grown to love it. We don't always get to make our own choices. Sometimes, some filthy fucker comes along and makes them for us, whether we want them to or not. I know one thing for certain now, though. No one will ever, ever, make a choice for me again, not when it's the monster who's in charge.

VIVIAN KASLEY hails from the land of the strange and unusual, Florida! She's a writer of short stories and poetry which have appeared in various science fiction anthologies, horror anthologies, horror magazines, and webzines. Some of her street cred includes Blood Bound Books, Dark Moon Digest, Gypsum Sound Tales, Ghost Orchid Press, Castrum Press, Hellbound Books, and most recently The Denver Horror Collective.

She's got more upcoming, including a tale in Vastarien, poetry in Black Spot Books inaugural women in horror poetry showcase: Under Her Skin, *and her very first novella.*

When not writing or subbing at the local middle school, she spends her time reading in bubble baths, snuggling her rescue cats and dogs, going on foodie dates with her other half, and searching for seashells and other treasures along the beach.

You can find her on Facebook @bizarrebabewhowrites, Amazon: amazon.com/author/viviankasley and Twitter @VKasley.

BLOOM

Alice Austin

I look up towards the top of the hill, where our friend Immy waits for us. I can already see some of the blooms from here; huge flowers, a mix of pink, brown, and red, swaying in the wind as we approach. Some of the ones with eyes turn to watch us climb. The sight sends a chill down my spine. No matter how noble and precious they are, I still find the whole idea grotesque; human flesh being twisted and used by these uncanny plants. By my side, Aisha can't stop gushing about how wonderful they are.

"Look at Joe's petals," she gasps, pointing at a huge pink flower with deep red veins forking through, dividing it into bold geometric sections visible even from a distance. "He's turned out so beautiful. I'm so happy for him. I hope I get flowers like that when I bloom."

"Mmmm," I say, unconvinced. I can sort of understand where she's coming from—the blooms are beautiful, in their own way. I just wish she wouldn't take every opportunity to turn the discussion towards them. She doesn't seem to realise that I don't love them quite as much as she does. "They're pretty, but I still don't like the idea of blooming! It just looks horrible and painful, and then you have to sit on the hill for the rest of your life doing nothing. I don't see what the appeal is."

"You will one day. I wasn't sure about them either, but when Immy bloomed, it was like something just… clicked in my head, and now it's all I want. You know what they say; it's instinctive. Our instinct to survive."

I roll my eyes. I wish she'd just listen to what I tell her every time she brings them up. I know they're vital to our survival. Without the blooms, the curse would fall upon our land and all our crops would wither and die. The strange beasts that roam the land would come rushing into our unprotected town, and everyone would die.

I understand the sacred nature of the flowers. I understand that blooming isn't as agonising as it looks, the plant pumping a rush of hormones into your veins that send you into a blissful daze throughout the prolonged, visceral process. I understand that it won't take away who you are as a person; if anything, it'll make you better, make you the person you were always meant to be.

That still doesn't mean I want to live tethered to the ground, with vines growing out of my eye sockets and roots embedded in my bones.

We reach the top of the hill. I can see Immy's slender, swaying form through a maze of fleshy vines and leaves. Aisha stops walking and turns to face me, suddenly serious.

"Speaking of blooming, I'm going back to the forest tomorrow," she says. "I didn't find a sapling last time, but I'm not going to give up. Will you come with me?"

"Sure." The forest is dangerous and I don't like going, but I'd never forgive myself if she went on her own and something bad happened to her. I try hard to push down the sadness which wells up at the thought of a sapling rooting itself into her flesh, integrating into her body. I know it won't change anything. After all, Immy's still Immy, even after she bloomed, but I'd be lying if I said it was exactly the same. It's like there's an invisible wall between us now; a boundary which I'll never be able to cross unless I become like her. We used to be so close, still are in a way, but it's not the same.

It'd break my heart if the same thing happened with Aisha. But this is her choice, and I have to respect it.

We resume walking, calling out greetings to the blooms we recognise. Some of them call back to us with the mouths they've managed to keep, others wave hand-shaped leaves as we pass. Eventually we reach Immy.

"Hey! So glad to see you both!" Immy beams down at us from above. She's about eight feet tall, elongated and skinny. Her vines wrap around me and Aisha in a hug. I smile, but my eyes are fixed on the line of tiny tan buds spouting down her spine. She leans back to her full height, revealing the bloody red cluster of flowers across her chest.

I'm probably biased because she's my friend, but Immy's bloom is the most beautiful of all of them. She looks like some sort of primal nature goddess, adorned with flowers. Some of the others look like scraggly bushes, thorny and ugly. I'd hate to go through all that just to end up as some twisted little thing overshadowed by the beauty all around me.

"Immy, your back!" Aisha squeals. "Can I have a look?"

"Sure!" Immy leans forwards again. I notice the skin around the buds is bulging with thick subcutaneous roots. "They started growing last week, apparently. I wouldn't know! I can't turn far enough to see. But it's exciting, anyway! By the way, do you have any water?" I step forwards and empty my water bottle over Immy's roots. She sighs with relief as it sinks into the fertile soil around her. It's warm today. She'll probably need us to bring her several more bottles of water while we're here.

Aisha spends more time cooing over Immy's new buds, while I sit quietly with a polite smile on my face. I love spending time with the pair of them, but it seems like the blooms are all they ever talk about anymore and it's just not something I can connect with. Sometimes it feels like I'm losing them to the flowers.

I wake up early the next morning to prepare. Thick trousers, long socks. I can't risk them riding up to expose an ankle. A turtleneck shirt, long enough to pull up and over my chin. Finally, a balaclava. Aisha laughs when she sees me.

"You look ridiculous!"

"Not as ridiculous as you'll look with flowers sprouting out your butt," I retaliate. "I'm not risking one of those things getting its roots in me."

"They will *not* sprout out of my butt!" Aisha replies, offended. I smirk, and with that we're off. It's a short walk to the giant, sprawling forest that surrounds and protects our village.

As we get further in, we start seeing wild blooms—thick luscious bushes with deep red heart-shaped leaves and no flowers. Aisha runs towards each one we see, plunging her arms into the foliage and rooting around before withdrawing them. I stand back expectantly, ready to console her each time her arms come back bare. I'm sure she'll find one eventually, and hopefully I can be a good friend and feign happiness when she does.

After hours of searching, she's still found nothing, and the sun is beginning to set.

"We should head home," I tell her hesitantly. She won't like to hear it, but it's not safe to be here after dark.

"Just one more bush," she pleads.

"We've checked all the bushes around here. It'll take ages to find another one. We need to go before it gets dark." Her face darkens.

"I know you hate the blooms, but this is what I want," she snaps. "We've got plenty of time to try once more. You're just worried that this will be the one."

I stare at her, shocked momentarily into silence. This isn't like her. Before I can even defend myself, she turns around and runs off.

"Shit. Aisha, wait!" I run after her, catching my foot on a root and sprawling into a bramble. I extract myself painfully, thorns tearing at my clothes and skin, and keep chasing her.

I find her kneeling by a bush we've already checked, arms deep in the tangle of branches and leaves. She pulls them out and sighs with disappointment.

"Aisha…" I begin, walking slowly towards her.

"I'm sorry about what I said," she says, straightening up. "I didn't mean it. You're supporting me by just being here. It's just so frustrating. I've been coming out here for months now, all for nothing. It feels like…" her voice fades away to nothing as she turns around to face me, eyes widening with shock. She raises a hand and points. "Maya, your arm."

I look down and my blood freezes as I see the tiny plant fixed to my arm, roots worming themselves through the rip in my sleeve. They've already entered my skin, blood crusted around where they've entered, flesh parting around them to allow the invader access to my body. I can see the veins in the leaf swelling and turning red as the plant connects to my own veins, my own heart betraying me and pumping my blood off to a parasite.

Time seems to slow down, the few brief seconds of staring stretching out into infinity. My stomach churns at the thought of roots penetrating my organs, leaching nutrients from my body. Buds erupting from my skin, bones rearranging themselves to whatever shape the plant feels is appropriate. Flowers forcing their way out of my mouth. Spending the rest of my life on that hill with all the other blooms. It's a great honour, but the thought makes me feel sick. I don't want this. I want a normal life. I want to fall in love and get married and have children.

"Shit. No. No."

Before I know it, I'm grabbing the sapling with my free hand, ready to wrench it out of my arm and toss it to the floor. I don't care how much it'll hurt, if the roots will shred my flesh as they exit. I just want this thing, this *intruder* out of my body. Aisha lunges forwards, gripping my wrist.

"Maya, no! What are you doing? You'll kill it!"

"I don't want it," I almost sob, straining against her. "I'll pull it off and we can put it on your arm and we'll both have what we want!"

"Are you crazy? You know that won't work. It won't survive that. Just calm down and think about it for a minute. I know it's a shock but..."

"I don't want it! You know I've never wanted this. I'll just rip it out and throw it back in the bush if you can't take it. We don't have to tell anyone. You won't tell anyone, will you?" I stare pleadingly at her. Aisha gasps.

"You can't rip it out! Maya, I know this isn't what you wanted but you can't suggest such horrible things. Come on. Let's go back home, and we can sit down and let you calm down a bit. It might not seem like it right now, but this is a good thing!" She slowly moves my arm away from the sapling and threads it through her own, gently guiding me forward. I follow, resisting the urge to break free and tear the thing from my arm. Maybe she's right. Maybe I'll come around. But for now, I can't stop thinking of the plant pulling my bones into new shapes and sinking roots into my blood vessels.

Everyone reacts with elation when they see the sprout on my arm. My parents hug me and tell me they're proud of me. People I've never spoken to approach to congratulate me. Everyone seems to assume I'm as happy about this as they are.

No matter how hard I try, I can't convince myself this is a good thing. Maybe there's something missing inside me. I remember what Aisha said about instinct; there must be something wrong with me. I'm missing that instinct, and that's why I can't connect with the flowers like the rest of them.

Weeks pass. The growing roots send pain shooting through my arm on a regular basis. I'm constantly hungry and exhausted, my body struggling to satisfy both itself and the parasite latched on to me. My shoulder itches and aches, the bulging of my flesh suggesting a leaf is about to burst free. Part of me is longing for this to end, the other part dreading what will come afterwards. This isn't right. I didn't want this, and I still don't.

Sometimes I still think about ripping the sapling from my body, but it's too late. The roots are so deeply entrenched I'd probably cause irreparable damage to my arm. Besides, it's common knowledge now. People have pulled out their unwanted blooms before, and though nobody will stop you, the disapproval will stick to you for life. I remember an old classmate, Lena, who ripped out her bloom about six weeks in. One of the roots had tapped into a vein in her neck and she almost bled to death. When she recovered, people smiled and nodded and said they understood. It was a big commitment, and her wellbeing was the most important thing. But behind her back it was all shock and disappointment about the way she'd acted; how could she carelessly destroy something so precious? Every time I think about tearing it out I remember how people treated her, and Aisha's reaction when I tried.

This bloom is a part of me now, whether I like it or not.

The only benefit is that Immy, Aisha, and I are inseparable now. I thought Aisha would be jealous and maybe even resentful, but she's ecstatic. All she ever talks about now is how me, her and Immy can be closer than ever. I sit with them both on the hill, supposedly celebrating, and listen to her talk.

"I was worried you'd get lonely when I end up here with Immy and you're just in the village on your own," she babbles. "This is perfect! I'm so glad you're feeling better about the whole thing now, Maya. I was worried about you to begin with." I force a fake smile and say nothing. I think there's a vine growing around the base of my tongue.

"I'll have to hurry up and get one myself," Aisha continues, oblivious. "Then maybe we can both move up here at the same time. That'd be amazing!"

"Aisha," Immy interrupts. "Would you get me some water?" I notice then that her leaves are starting to droop. It's a hot day. She must be parched.

"Of course!" Aisha grabs a bottle and jogs off towards the tap located just outside the cluster of blooms. Immy watches her go, a smile on her lengthened face. The smile fades as she looks down at me.

“Are you really okay with this, Maya? You never wanted to bloom before, and I know how Aisha tends to see what she wants to see. To me you don’t seem happy.” I glance around us, wary of all the blooms around that might be listening to our conversation.

“No,” I say in a lowered voice, my voice cracking. “I hate this. I wish I could tear it out and give it to Aisha. But what can I do? It’s too late to rip it out.” Immy sighs.

“I thought as much. I’m sorry, Maya. I don’t know what to suggest.”

“Maybe I should cut my arm off,” I say gloomily. Even that probably won’t work. I think I can feel a pioneering root squirming its way through my rib cage. Once it reaches my heart, there really will be no turning back. Immy shakes her head.

“You can’t go through with this, that’s for sure.” I stare at her, open-mouthed. Of all the people, I hadn’t expected Immy to be the one to sympathise with my blasphemous thoughts.

“Wha—” I start.

“Don’t get me wrong, I’m so glad I chose to do this. I love it. The sun really makes you feel alive. The rain is nourishing rather than depressing, and I know that I’m helping everyone in the village. But it’s not for everyone, and if it’s not something you want, it must be a horrendous experience. I don’t blame Lena for what she did, and I expect she’s glad she did it. You might be able to uproot it without harming yourself, but it might be too late. I really don’t know what to say other than I’m sorry. And I’m always here if you need to talk.” I feel tears prick my eyes.

"Thank you Immy," I mumble. She wraps her vines around me in a hug.

"I'm sorry if I've been distant since I bloomed," she says. "It really changes the way you look at the world. It's like… oh, hi Aisha! Thank you so much." I lean back and fix that same dead smile on my face as Aisha pours out her bottle of water on Immy's roots. Looking at it makes me feel thirsty, so I pull out my own water bottle for a drink. And stop.

I can feel the roots in my arm pulsing with anticipation, the wilting leaves on my arm practically begging me to drink. The bloom is thirstier than I am. Instead of taking a swig, I unscrew the top of my bottle and pour it out over Immy.

"Sorry Aisha," I say. "I forgot I already had some water I could've given her."

I get back home, go into our sunny garden, and start running laps. Sweat drips from my brow and pain shoots through my arm and torso as the bloom puts out new roots, desperately searching for more water in my system. I cruelly deny it this privilege. I know what I'm doing is risky; it could drain all the water from my blood, but I don't think it will. The parasite can't afford to kill its host.

Bloody leaves droop. I sweat. Thin, hair-like roots erupt from the soles of my feet, trying to dig their way into the parched soil in a desperate bid for moisture. I cut the roots with scissors, wincing as the pain shoots back into my own nerves. My head pounds and my mouth is dry. I choke on a root worming its way up the back of my throat, searching for any spare saliva to absorb. More leaves force their way from my skin, twisted and malformed into cones to funnel every drip of sweat back into my body where it can be drained. It's trying to prematurely bloom, push me past the point of no return so I can't kill it without also killing myself. A vine erupts from my heel, twisting up and around my leg, throwing me off balance. I fall to the floor but jump back up and keep moving, limping as fast as I can as buds sprout from my shoulders. If they bloom, it's all over. I keep running until I can't run any longer and collapse to the floor, weak and dizzy. I crawl back inside, into my bed, and pass out.

"Maya! Are you alright?" A voice pierces through the darkness and silence. I can feel something cool and soothing touch my lips. I open my mouth instinctively and swallow, before my brain catches up and tells me I shouldn't be drinking. My eyes snap open and I push the glass of water away, scrambling for safety.

I fucked up; I killed the bloom, and now the curse has come to our village. The beasts have broken through the walls and I made it happen. I was so selfish. This is all my fault...

"Hey, slow down! You're really dehydrated. You need to…" I slowly come around to reality and realise there are no beasts. The grass has not shrivelled and died. Everything is fine. I ignore Aisha's pleading and look at my shoulder. My vision is blurry at first, but the bud comes into focus quickly. It's brown and shrivelled. I reach out to touch the withered leaves on my arm, and they break free and drift down to the floor. Aisha sighs.

"I'm so sorry Maya. I got someone to come and take a look at it for you, but it's dead."

"Oh no," I say, trying my best to sound convincing. Aisha's eyes brim with tears and she throws her arms around me.

"I know this must be horrible for you," she whispers. I say nothing, letting her believe whatever she needs to believe. Inside, relief is crashing through me like a tidal wave, strong enough to bring tears to my eyes. I'm not going to bloom. I don't have to give up my body and my life for this thing I never wanted, and the village isn't going to suffer for it.

It doesn't matter what people think of me now. Immy was right. I could never have gone through with this.

ALICE AUSTIN is an author of horror and fantasy – the weirder and creepier the better. She and her partner share their home in Kent, UK with an adorable menace of a cat. Find her on Twitter at @Al_Austin120.

BLESSED ART THOU AMONG WOMEN

Vashelle Nino

Christina studied the tall figurine of the Virgin Mary perched on the particle board bookshelf across the room. Her robes draped over her body like a thin sheet of fondant over a silky white cake. A blue cincture with golden tassels tied around her waist accentuated an hourglass figure. Little knick-knacks surrounded her like adoring children during story-time: a lighter, loose change, two beer bottle caps, and a little remote for the oscillating fan. The Virgin seemed to stare back. Stare *through.*

A thunderous voice broke Christina's trance.

"All this body-positive bullshit. Pfft! The more you girls holler 'Self-love!' the more you're using filters and contouring yourselves like pinche pendejas."

Ms Ortiz was never one to hold back. She'd filet your deepest insecurities, salt your most painful wound, and serve it to you like sizzling fajitas on an iron skillet.

She continued, "When we were your age we didn't give a fuck about any of that. The guys got what they got. We didn't highlight our noses or wax our moustaches. Shit, we didn't wax down there either. Do you think that stopped any of us from sitting on a face? Ahhh haaaaa!"

"Oh god, mom! Stop!" Andrea protested.

Christina giggled. She always loved Ms Ortiz's directness. When she and Andrea were younger, she wished her own mother could be a little more like her best friend's mom and less like the pious Virgin staring at her from the shelf. She didn't feel that way anymore. She recognised the ways Ms Ortiz had to pay for her vulgarity. She'd been fired from countless jobs, lost plenty of friends, and struggled to keep a man in her life. Nonetheless, Christina loved visiting with her when she was in town between semesters.

"Anyways, mom. Leave me and my contouring alone."

"And your fake-ass eyelashes."

The three of them laughed.

Andrea put her phone away and wondered why she thought asking her mom to take a picture of them would go without its share of ball-busting.

"Alright. We're heading out. Don't wait up for me."

Ms Ortiz took a swig of her Shiner and nodded.

Andrea and Christina each gave her a kiss on the cheek and marched out of the meagre apartment on Green Street.

"Your mom is right," Christina said as they walked to the car.

"About what?"

"About the contouring and filters and all that shit. Think about it. When was the last time you posted a picture of yourself without a filter?"

Andrea contemplated.

"Exactly."

"But *everyone* is fucking flawless now. How do you even compete without that all extra shit?"

"Compete for what, though? Someone's bum of a son? Anyway, God himself knocked up The Virgin and I guarantee you that bitch wasn't doing chemical peels."

Andrea gave Christina the side eye and then they laughed, and, in unison—like they used to do at Sunday mass after a sleepover at Christina's—they motioned the sign of the cross for forgiveness.

"Well, you know my mom. She's never wrong."

"Yeah," Christina said, resigned. "You got a lighter?"

Andrea pulled a Zippo from her loose pocket and handed it to her.

"Light up."

In bed later that night, Christina studied all the familiar faces on Instagram and the way they'd changed. Change was expected, yes. They weren't kids anymore. But the unnatural backsides, pointier noses, fuller lips. She couldn't stop thinking about what Ms Ortiz said and how remiss something must be for their collective words not to match their actions, and how oblivious they were not to even realise it. She tried to remember what it was like before. She couldn't. Was it ever *not* like this for them?

The guys got what they got. Never stopped us from sitting on a face.

Christina chuckled to herself and put her phone on the nightstand.

Fuck this, she thought. *I refuse to be like everyone else.*

As she drifted to sleep, still a little high from earlier, images of the Virgin flickered in her mind like a shorted light: a vibrant mural of the Blessed Mother she saw in downtown Phoenix once; the faded garden statue of *La Virgen de Guadalupe* in the front of her grandparents' meagre house; the detailed forearm tattoo on the guy who tried to force himself on her at a party when she was seventeen; the Hail Holy Queen charm on her mother's cherished rosaries.

Someone called Christina's name, soft and enticing, and in that moment she found herself pulled back into the thick living room of Ms Ortiz's apartment. Except this time she was alone.

Christina, it called.

Christina. Over here.

Struck by a certain degree of lucidity, she suddenly remembered the figurine on the bookshelf from earlier. She walked toward it.

Come closer, mi amor, it said.

Nothing about the figurine was moving. Neither its mouth nor its body. Still, Christina knew it was the source of the voice calling her name. She remembered the joke she'd cracked earlier and felt uneasy.

"Mother of God, I—"

Sweet girl. Tell me what's on your heart.

She had trouble discerning the figurine's motives. On one hand, it was the Mother of Mercy, her Immaculate Heart dripping in love and grief, passion and forgiveness; on the other, something in her voice had a whisper of cunning. *Impossible,* she thought. *It's Our Lady.*

She heard Ms Ortiz's voice in her mind: *...contouring yourselves like pinche pendejas.*

"I want to be free, Mother."

How do you mean, child?

"Free to be myself. Natural. Uninhibited. Free of expectations and envy."

And how do we do that?

"Without makeup and filters. Without obsessing over my body and what I'm eating or how many steps and squats I got in by the end of the day. I want to be liked for being different, for being *me.*"

And who are you?

"I'm *me.* Christina. I'm not like everyone else. Not deep inside."

You're special, aren't you? Smarter.

"Well, aren't we all? God made us all in his image, but different. Except everyone's conforming to something, one way or another."

And you know better.

"I think so."

Very well, sweet child. When you awake, you will no longer conform. Your current insecurities will vanish and people will recognise you for what you are: different. No more makeup. No more filters. No more—her voice began to change—*ego.*

The Virgin's face began contorting, resembling the faces of demons Christina's mother showed her when she was little, to scare her into submission. Her modest robes sloughed away and her wicked body enticed, naked. The cunning undertones Christina recognised at the beginning grew full-blown diabolical.

Didn't you pay any attention in Sunday school, Christina? "Do nothing from rivalry or conceit, but in humility count others more significant than yourselves." Philippians 2:3. You're no different. Being different for the sake of being different is still vanity. "Everyone who is arrogant in heart is an abomination to the Lord; be assured, he will not go unpunished."

It loved desecrating the Lord's word and exploiting it for the quandary it was. The voice revelled so loudly, Christina's head rang. She willed herself awake.

It was just a nightmare, she thought, relieved but drained. Her face ached a little. She figured she'd been wincing in her sleep. The sweat seeping onto her forehead seemed to burn.

She reached for her phone on the nightstand and, out of habit, hit the Instagram icon. It was the last photo she'd seen before falling asleep, so she refreshed the page. A new photo took its place: The Virgin figurine from Ms Ortiz's. *Sponsored,* from an account she'd never heard of. The caption read: *Pride goes before destruction, and a haughty spirit before a fall.*

She quickly shut off her phone, jolted up, and turned on her nightstand lamp.

What the fuck? Am I still asleep?

She reached for her phone again, but this time she screamed at the sight of her raw, deformed face reflected in the black screen.

A sweet, deceitful voice taunted: *When you awake you will no longer conform. Your current insecurities will vanish and people will recognise you for what you are: different. No more makeup. No more filters. No more ego.*

VASHELLE NINO's writing is influenced by her life as a third generation Mexican-American Army brat who lived in nine states and abroad before the age of thirty; as well as her innate interests in the human shadow, taboo, and macabre—especially that which contain religious or mystical undertones. You can find her on Twitter, Instagram and TikTok as @Vashelle_Writes or on her website: www.vashellewrites.com.

THE GLOBE

Cecilia Kennedy

Poking at my bloated belly, I feel bubbles of air rippling just below the surface. I've come to know this part of me as The Globe—sticking out from under my shirts, pants, pushed back beneath shaping garments. Sometimes I think I could prick it with a pin, and water and globules of gelatine-like pieces would ooze out, and I'd feel so much better.

Budding continents spread across The Globe. There's the Appendectomy Surgical Scar Equator Line which, after just one pregnancy, grew fingers that reached around to my backside and pointed south. There's Gummy Bear Pole and the South Soda Sea. The Globe is something I'd change, if I could change just one thing.

"Why do you pinch your stomach like that?" my five-year-old daughter asks.

"I think part of you is still in there," I say, smiling.

"Then, you should love it," she says.

I wrap my arms around her, but inside, I just don't love it. I want it gone.

Under bright lights, and amid the sterile smell of rubbing alcohol, I'm weighed in the doctor's office. According to the scale, I've gained ten pounds.

"All in my stomach," I tell the doctor. "And it's getting worse with age."

"Eat whole foods."

"I do, for the most part."

"Now, now. I'm sure you sneak in a few chips? Go to the drive-through?"

"Not really."

"And exercise. You should exercise."

"I do. Two hours a day. I'm sore and tired, and my legs and hips are cramping. I don't know how much longer I can take."

"Hmm."

"What about lipo?"

"How about I give you this pamphlet?"

And I leave with a booklet about how to lose weight with diet and exercise. I sit in my car, stretch The Globe, and write a nasty review online about the doctor who won't listen.

I go, against my doctor's wishes, to the cool sculpting and lipo centre in the strip mall near the fancy part of town.

"It's all too expensive," I tell the physician assistant.

"There *is* a new, experimental procedure that I think you could qualify for. It's free, but it hasn't been tested yet."

He tells me he'll insert a clear plastic tube into The Globe, and I will just walk around with it all day, for a month or so, but I can eat anything I want. The tube will drain the fat, naturally. He explains that it's environmentally sound because there won't be any waste to wrap up in plastic. My fat will simply mix into the earth and decompose when I'm walking around outside. Or, if I'm inside, I can unfasten the stopper at the end of the tube and drain it into biodegradable trays made of plant material.

After I sign a waiver, I go into the surgical procedures room. The physician assistant numbs a small area of The Globe, right below my navel. He inserts the tube, and I watch as a thick, creamy yellow fluid, tinged with red, runs through. Already I think I see The Globe deflating.

Over time, The Globe shrinks to nothing more than an almost-imperceptible ping-pong ball. Solidified pieces of yellow fat get stuck between pockets of air in the tube. They flatten against the sides, hardening like delicate crusted webs.

When I go back to the lipo centre, I tell the physician assistant that I'm happy with the results, and that I'm ready to have the tube pulled. On the examination table, I recline while the assistant pokes and tugs gently on the tube, but then he stops and tells me to sit up. There's an ultrasound machine in the building next door, and he's making an appointment for me now. Something is wrong.

The ultrasound technician turns a monitor towards me, and the physician assistant points to the screen.

“This is the abdominal aorta,” he says. “The tube has somehow fused itself to this major blood vessel. If I remove the tube, the vessel will burst, and you will die.”

“So what happens now?”

“We’ll just leave it in.”

“Forever?”

“Forever.”

At home, I go to the upstairs bathroom. My five-year-old follows me inside.

“Watcha’ doin’, Mommy?”

“Oh, just seeing if I can snip this tube back a little.”

I have the scissors from the downstairs drawer, and I cut the tube as close as I can to my stomach, but I leave a little bit that sticks out, just in case. My daughter watches me, breathing steadily, and I wonder what will happen if I pull on the edge of the tube that’s still sticking out. When I do, I feel a rushing gush of fluid that flows up through the part that’s still inside me. Out the other end it comes, along with a ping-pong ball sized globule, covered in blood.

“Is that the part of me that’s been stuck inside of you, Mommy?”

“Why, yes. I think it is. And I think I’ll keep it safe.”

I wrap the knobby gristle and flesh in a tissue and bring it back downstairs to the kitchen, along with the longer tube I’ve cut. My daughter follows me. From the cupboard, I select a glass jar and drop the globule inside.

“Mommy, more of me is coming out of you,” my daughter says.

And when I look at my stomach, I see blood, thick and spreading, pouring through my clothes and onto the linoleum. I steady myself by holding onto the kitchen countertop, and I gaze at my daughter, looking into her scared, sad eyes. Into a freezer-sized plastic bag, I manage to drop the tube I've cut. I reach out to her, holding it.

"This is yours, my dear. In case you ever need it."

Her body grows rigid, defiant; her face turns red.

"I won't wear it, Mommy! I won't!" she says, knocking the jar that holds a part of her from the counter—sending it, in a storm of shrieks and oily shards, crashing to the floor.

CECILIA KENNEDY taught English and Spanish courses in Ohio before moving to Washington state and publishing short stories in various magazines and anthologies. The Places We Haunt *is her first short story collection. You can find her DIY humour blog and other adventures/achievements here: https://fixinleaksnleeksdiy.blog/. She can also be found on Twitter: @ckennedyhola.*

HYSTERICAL

Lindsay King-Miller

The woman in the mirror has warm brown eyes and round cheeks. She isn't me; I've known it for weeks now. I don't have that slight smile at the corner of my mouth. I'm sallow and thin with bags under my eyes.

I stare her dead in the face, waiting to catch her blinking out of sync with me, but she doesn't, or maybe can't. It's hard to tell whether mimicry is an act she's practiced to perfection or a fate she can't escape.

She flinches just like I do when the timer on my phone goes off. We've been watching each other like this for three minutes. I know what the piece of plastic will say before I even look at it: I'm not pregnant. Just like last month, and the month before that, and all seventeen of the months before that.

The woman in the mirror looks at me with wide eyes. I can't tell if her expression is shock or sorrow. I wipe the pregnancy test with a wad of toilet paper and shove it into my pocket. The last thing I need is for my employer to discover it in her trash.

Outside the door, the children shout over each other, competing for my attention. I'm a nanny for Mrs Hale. She works from home, offering telehealth therapy appointments from her office, which is a separate room from her bedroom. While she's in there with the door closed, I'm in charge of Logan and Everett. They argue and snap at each other all day. It's exhausting. I think it's the strangeness of knowing their mother is right down the hall, but unavailable to them. They miss her even though she's in the house.

I open the door, and Logan immediately swarms up my legs. Everett wants a graham cracker. I do whatever they ask me to do, go where they want me to go, and try not to look them in the eyes. I don't want to love anything I can't keep.

At home, I shower off the day, the invisible marks sticky hands have left on my body. In the shower, long strands of my hair come away in my fingers. I let them swirl down the drain. Maybe I'll move before it needs to be snaked. I'm losing more and more of it, from stress or disappointment or not enough to eat, the flaking skin of my scalp showing through.

I climb out and stand dripping wet before the foggy mirror. Water puddles and quickly cools on the tile beneath my feet. I bare my teeth at the woman in the mirror, a grey silhouette who could almost be mistaken for me. I can't tell if she returns my grimace.

Her face is rounder than it used to be, her breasts heavier. I think she might be pregnant. I've taken three more tests and I know I'm not, but the despair I feel with every consecutive negative is never there in her eyes. Even though I can't see the expression on her face, she looks happy. I can't stand it.

In the morning, her hair is a tangled mess from going to bed without drying it, but it still looks good. She's not losing it the way I am; hers is glossy and lustrous. I remember reading that pregnancy can change the colour and texture of your hair. I grab a strand of my own and pull it in front of my face, trying to compare the colour. She does the same thing, mocking me.

I twist the strand around my forefinger and yank, hard. The sound of ripping is, for one blinding moment, worse than the pain. The lock of hair comes away in my hand, and I stare at it, then in the mirror. Blood beading at my hairline. My reflection's wide, startled eyes, like a woodland animal staring at a gun for the first time.

I grab another strand of hair and yank it out again. The pain is bright and satisfying, like peeling a scab. Beneath my hair, the skin is so tender, a soft part of my body I've never looked at closely before. A few sharp spurts of blood speckle the mirror, but mostly it wells slow and thin, meandering in creeks and rivulets across my scalp. I rip and rip and watch my reflection's eyes fill with tears.

When I stop, my hair is a wild mess of clumps and bare patches, and the sink is half-full of torn-out locks. There are scissors in the kitchen drawer. I carry them back to the bathroom held out before me, point up, the way I tell Logan and Everett not to.

Leaning over the sink, I use the scissors to hack through what remains of my hair. My hand starts to hurt by the time I'm halfway done. Little pieces of hair stick to my forehead and my ears, cling to the bloody stretches of my scalp. I see that my reflection works with the tip of her tongue between her teeth, just like I do, and for a moment I have the strong urge to clamp my jaw shut as hard as I can, see if I can bite it off.

But the desire passes. It's enough to feel the muscles in my hand burn from the steady, repetitive motion of opening and closing the scissors; to hear the sound of hair landing on porcelain like sporadic rain. I can't see the back of my head, so I just keep cutting until the blades are scraping the skin. When I'm done, my hair is ragged and ugly, the skin raw in places where I went too short, and the scissors are probably ruined. My reflection looks small and confused with her pretty hair gone. It serves her right.

I wonder if she's picked out names for the baby yet. I've never let myself think that far ahead.

After work, I get out the scissors again, but I don't cut my hair this time. I just stand there looking in the mirror, my tongue between my teeth, opening and closing the blades and listening to the gritting metal sound. I put my index finger between the dull blades of the scissors and squeeze the handles together. The pressure hurts, but it's not enough to break the skin.

Instead, I jam the pointed beak into the flesh of my upper arm, hard and fast, like administering myself an injection. I do it over and over, five times, ten. It leaves red welts that don't bleed.

I drop the scissors and stare at my reflection. She looks confused, but not pained. Never afraid. Nothing seems to bother her.

I let my head fall back between my shoulders, indulge myself for one moment in a wail of quiet despair. I wonder what sound my double would make if I could hear her. My hands tighten on the edge of the sink, and then, before I can talk myself out of it, I whip my head forward and slam my face into the mirror.

There's a crunching sound and a bright, silvery wave of pain. For a moment I can't see anything except red.

When my vision clears, I can tell that what broke was my nose, not the glass. That's probably the better of the two options. Blood runs from my nostrils, pooling in the divot of my upper lip before spilling down over my mouth and chin. There's a red smear on the mirror in the middle of my reflection's face. She stares back at me, bleeding, and through the pain I feel a piercing thrill of triumph.

"What happened to your face?" Mrs Hale asks. It strikes me as a rude question.

"I hit it," I say. She stares at me. I stare back. Eventually she goes into her office, but she leaves the door open.

Everett wants to give his brother a haircut. I tell him where his mother keeps the scissors, up in the cupboard above the refrigerator. "I can't reach," he says.

"There's a stepladder in the basement," I tell him.

The brushed steel door of the Hales' refrigerator is shiny enough to see my reflection. Her eyes are larger than usual under her sparse, scruffy hair. In the shadowy grey surface, they look black and bottomless as pits.

Everett starts back up the stairs, his footsteps echoed by the heavy thump of the ladder he's dragging behind him. Then the dragging stops, and I hear a scrape, a grunt. Logan says something to me, but I don't hear what it is. My eyes are still locked on my double's. There's a sound that reminds me of a stack of boxes toppling over, and then a scream.

I wonder how long it will take Mrs Hale, tucked away in her office, to notice that her child is hurt; to respond to his cries. He needs her. How can she not know that he needs her? If it were my baby, I think, I would know instantly. I'd be by his side before he even reached the bottom of the stairs. I stand in the kitchen, not moving.

After Mrs Hale bandages Logan's skinned elbow and fires me, I sit in my car in her driveway, watching the house. It's strange to think I'll never cross its threshold again. I can't remember most of what Mrs Hale screamed at me, and that's probably for the best. My reflection in the rear view mirror looks shell-shocked. I think she's taking this harder than I am. Losing her job might be the first really traumatic thing that's happened in her life.

It makes me angry the more I think about it—how surprised she is, as if the injustice is simply overwhelming. When is she going to stop sitting there with a stupid look on her face while life runs roughshod all over her? When is she going to stand up and fight for herself? She's expecting a baby; a mother can't afford to be a fainting flower. She has to be a beast, a fighter, willing to bite and claw and savage.

She and Mrs Hale don't understand about instinct, about devotion. They want to hide in their comfortable rooms and pretend motherhood is singing lullabies and posing for family portraits. I'm the one who knows it's a bloody, brutal mess.

I open the car door. Wrap my hand around the metal doorframe, just above my head. It takes a little stretching, but I reach across my body with my other arm and grab the door handle. Stare my reflection dead in the eyes. Slam the door shut with my entire weight.

I feel every bone that shatters in my fingers. The pain is huge and white and ugly and spilling over into every part of my body. I'm screaming, my body twisted into a parody of a self-embrace, my hand stuck in the door. There are layers to the agony: skin, muscle, bone. I open the door. Scream again. Blood pulsing out of my fingers in heartbeat spurts. I see bone.

Mrs Hale throws her front door open. "Samantha! What in the name—?" She doesn't finish her sentence, just stares at me.

I'm still screaming, can't stop screaming, will never stop screaming. I throw the car into reverse and screech out of the Hales' driveway. The door is still hanging open, but when I slam into drive, the momentum swings it shut.

I don't recognise the streets I'm driving on, even though I know this neighbourhood as well as my own. Know it like the back of my hand, I think, and then I sneak a look at the back of my left hand and my stomach snarls. Something stringy—a vein?—dangles from the base of my ring finger. There's a lot of blood. My pulse is so strong in my bruised and broken hand that I can hear it, a steady, sickening rhythm.

I drive through a traffic light and can't remember whether it was green or red. My hand hurts so much that everything else hurts too, echoes of pain from all over my body. The deepest, blackest pain is in my stomach. My guts twist like I'm going to shit my pants. When I look down, I see blood on my jeans, between my legs.

A siren blares behind me, flashing red and blue lights in the rear view mirror. Mrs Hale must have called them, or maybe it's because of the way I'm driving. "Fuck that," I snarl, and stomp on the gas pedal.

I'm still looking in the rear view and I don't even see the minivan in front of me until I'm halfway through it, my hood smashing and crumpling into the van's hatchback. My face rebounds off the airbag and there's a scorched, powdery smell. The pain in my hand swells like a balloon until it bursts, spilling everywhere. I'm drenched in blood and vomit and broken glass.

When they drag me from the wreckage, the people from the minivan are already out, standing by the side of the road. A man is holding a screaming baby. "Where is its mother?" I try to ask. My words come out jumbled, catching on unexpected gaps and sharp edges in my mouth—broken teeth. "The baby," I try again. "The baby needs its mother."

"Samantha?" How do they know my name? "Samantha, we're going to help your baby if we can, but we've got to get you stable first."

Not mine, I try to say, but the words get lost on their way to my lips.

Later, I'm in a bed. My left hand is huge, full of tubes putting things into it and taking things out, with bandages to hold all the tubes in place. People are talking. There was no way to save the pregnancy, a nurse tells me. Catastrophic trauma, someone says, and points to my hand.

"I was never pregnant," I try to explain. "It was her. This is her miscarriage, not mine," but no one understands.

Someone helps me to the bathroom. My face in the mirror is horrible, covered in bruises and blood, teeth missing, no hair. I look for the other one, a glimpse of my double. I want to see her with her world in ruins, staring at the annihilation of her life. But I can't find her anywhere. All I see is my own sad eyes looking back at me.

LINDSAY KING-MILLER is the author of Ask A Queer Chick: A Guide to Sex, Love, and Life for Girls who Dig Girls *(Plume, 2016). Her fiction has appeared in the anthologies* The Fiends in the Furrows *(Nosetouch, 2018),* Tiny Nightmares *(Catapult, 2020), and elsewhere. She lives in Denver with her partner and their two children.*

KNIT, PURL

Nicole M. Wolverton

Mrs Elmira McFadden unexpectedly passed away while in the middle of knitting a blanket for Jeannette Winterbaum's charity auction. It's a beautiful blanket—made from cashmere wool that Elmira had spun herself and dyed the colour of a coastal Stellar's jay flying in a clear blue sky. Elmira had created the design as well—two chunky cables running the length of the blanket, left and right, with a complicated Saxon braid winding its way down the middle.

"It's a shame it'll never be finished now." Lettie Wattley runs a crooked finger down the wide centre braid. She has the blanket spread out on the project table in the classroom space at the back of her yarn studio. The sunlight shines through the tall windows, highlighting the subtle variations in the yarn colour and making Lettie's red page boy cut glow fire.

"Why won't it be finished?" I push a light closer to the yarn to inspect it. Expertly spun. Elmira's skill never fails to impress. "I'm sure I can figure out this pattern. Maybe complete the row she was working on to finish out using her yarn—we could knit the second half of the blanket using something else and graft it together. Oh, we could include a stripe of a different colour to show the before and after. We could call it a life and death blanket. Very exclusive."

Lettie and her bright pink lipstick frown. "Elmira would find a way to reanimate and kill you if you tried such a thing, Quinn." She cocks her head. "Although if you think you can figure out the pattern, I do have all the yarn she spun for it. Her husband came by the other day and dropped off every blessed scrap of yarn and every needle in the house—he said he couldn't look at it anymore. Said he kept hearing her voice, muttering pattern changes."

"But he didn't bring the pattern?"

"Guess it didn't occur to him. Or maybe it looked like a doodle. You know how Elmira was about pattern-making." Lettie pauses. "But I bet you could do Elmira and her blanket design justice—you've got a real eye for this kind of thing. I'd love to see the project completed as intended."

"You know what?" I say. "I'll take it on. I've been looking for a nice way to honour Elmira. I was going to make a donation in her name to that hunger non-profit she liked so much, but this is even better. More personal."

"I daresay that with a story like this, that blanket will raise an enormous amount of money, too." Lettie nods approvingly. "The gala is in about three weeks. Think you can make the deadline?"

"Ooooo, that's not a lot of time, is it?" I eye the cables, the intricacy as they loop back on each other. "But yeah, if I do nothing but knit on the project after work, yeah. I think I can make it happen."

Before the final words come out of my mouth, Lettie bustles into the storage closet and emerges with a bright orange plastic bag bulging with squat blue cakes of yarn. She hands me the bag and folds the blanket. "Thank god Hank didn't yank out the circular needles. You'd have had a hell of a time sorting out the stitches."

"I can't get over this colour. What do you think she used for dye?"

"No idea. She usually went in for naturals and organics, but I've never seen anything that would produce this particular colour. Mind your hands as you're knitting, in case it's not set fast—can't imagine your third graders would leave that well enough alone. A teacher with blue hands! Granted, can't imagine Elmira doing anything half-assed, so you're probably fine, but you never know." She smiles. "And thanks. Really. I'm so thrilled."

The funeral comes the very next day. I pack a half-finished sock project in my bag for the occasion. A vibrant blood-red wool. Reverend Hunsinger can get worked up when a parishioner dies—and idle hands are supposed to be the devil's work and all that. He'd come to terms with us knitting during his sermons years ago. At the funeral, the group of us who knit together at Lettie's shop sit together in the dark wood pews, a tight clot of us, minding not to click our needles too loudly as the stained glass windows cast a rainbow over us.

Brenda, the newest of us and the youngest at twenty-six, sits next me, knitting one, purling two across a pretty merino wool scarf. The colour reminds me of dandelions. Her stitches are careful and slow. She nudges me. "How did Elmira die? No one's said."

"She's had very high blood pressure for years," I murmur, and count out my stitches for a heel flap. "Apparently she was in her favourite chair, knitting a blanket, and she just—*bang*—had a stroke. She was gone just like that. Painless. Peaceful. It's the way we should all go when it's our time."

She huffs. "You say that like it's coming up for you—you're only ten years older than I am. Elmira was an old woman."

I nearly laugh. Brenda is a long-limbed, willowy girl with an arresting face and close-shorn brown hair. I never looked like that at her age. "I mean *collectively* our time."

She's quiet for a moment. "I thought maybe it had to do with those terrible veins in her legs."

Elmira's legs were a squiggly roadmap of blue and purple cords as thick as a pencil. Her veins scared the crap out of me. I always wondered what they felt like. They looked hard, like they'd roll under her skin like electrical cables. "I don't think so. I mean, I think she had some pain from her varicose veins, but nothing as bad as that—she's had them... I think she said since her second pregnancy."

"I have to tell you—the more I hear about being pregnant and giving birth, the less I think it's a good idea."

"Preaching to the choir," I say. "Everything about it sounds horrifying."

I'm still thinking of Elmira's legs by the time I get home from the service. The heel on my blood-red sock is turned, and I knitted nearly all the way to the toe. But now is not the time for socks—I sit at my kitchen table and unfold Elmira's bird-blue blanket to start charting out her stitches. Come to think of it, the blue yarn that she's spun is nearly the colour I envision when I remember her varicose veins. Now that I've made the connection, the blanket seems depressing and terrible. Still beautiful, though, in the strangest and most unappealing way.

Elmira wasn't one to hide her veins like other women did. She hated them and always talked about having surgery to correct them, but she never did. One day at Lettie's shop, I was sitting next to her in the classroom. I was sure I could see those veins writhing under her skin like an angry snake. She'd seen me looking and patted my hand.

"You'll probably have them one day," she'd said. "They'll come for you. As knitters, we sit a lot, and that's what they love. Maybe you'll have a baby—that sometimes brings them on—or maybe you'll get them in menopause. It certainly made mine worse. But those veins, they'll come for you."

I abruptly stand and shake out my legs. Tap my bare toes a few times on the cold, scuffed linoleum. My nervous laughter echoes off the white kitchen walls. Shadows collect in the corners of the room—it's getting darker earlier these days. I lean over the table and keep counting and recounting, configuring the chart. I'm sure I've cracked Elmira's cables and her braid. All I have to do is test my guesstimated pattern and match my knitting gauge to hers.

Elmira's abrupt voice reverberates in my ear. "They'll come for you."

I shudder and pick out a set of needles from my stash, fish a cake of Elmira's cashmere from the orange bag. It must have taken her months to spin it all. Months of sitting at her wheel, drafting up her singles… the plying and dying and blocking and winding. All while those terrible veins throbbed in her legs, day and night.

My kitchen was never the biggest room in my house—large enough for me, though. I don't need much. A little counter space, a refrigerator and stove. Just enough room for a small table. I pace the length of the room as I knit—step, knit, step, knit, step, knit, step, slip three stitches purl-wise onto a holder, step, knit, step, knit, step, knit the holder stitches. Back and forth—the cables, the braid, and then more cables. The shadows grow longer. I keep pacing. Elmira's voice in my head screams louder. I knit faster. Finally, I sample to measure gauge. It's only then that her voice quiets, and still I imagine the veins in my own legs grow larger, harder.

My gauge is a perfect match to Elmira's—and my fingertips have turned blue from the dye in her yarn, just as Lettie warned.

Maybe it was being in communion with Elmira's blanket for so many hours, or the constant reminder of her on my fingertips—I cannot get her voice out of my head. "They'll come for you," always seems to be repeating, over and over again, no matter what. When I'm teaching. At recess. While knitting Elmira's cables and braids. And at night I dream.

It's the same dream every night. The veins come, first as a heavy, needful ache deep in my legs. My muscles cramp and burn. And then thick blue ropes surface. They bulge up, pulsing and screaming my name. Winding themselves over my calves like country roads, stitching across my knees and spiralling haphazardly around my thighs. The veins burst through my skin and shoot out sucker veins, anchoring me to the bed, the wall, the floor, wherever I am until I'm nothing more than an incubator, feeding blood to the veins that imprison me in a useless body.

My screams are loud enough to wake me. My legs itch as though ants pinch and crawl, and I turn on the bedside light and scratch until the sensation passes.

I take the blanket to Lettie's shop a week after Elmira's funeral, as much for the company of our knitting group as to show off the progress I've made. Brenda gushes over how exactly I've continued the blanket. I smile but stay quiet—she has yet to move on from her simple yellow scarf. Everything seems amazing to her.

"It's a shame about the dye." Lettie sets down a glass teapot on the project table.

"I thought about trying to re-fix the dye—you know, cake by cake, but it seems less time intensive to fix it when the blanket is complete. I can soak it in vinegar in my tub and then block it afterwards."

Lettie nods. "That could work. If it doesn't, maybe just give it a good wash in dish detergent to remove the excess dye. Same thing—then you can block it. Feel free to use the project table here. Or do you have the space at your apartment?"

"No, I'll do it here. Thanks for the offer." I scratch my ankle through the bandage I'd put on after last night's dream.

Brenda glances down, and her eyes widen. "What happened to your leg, Quinn? It looks like it went through the meat grinder."

I flap my hand at her. Blood is crusted under my short nails. "Nothing—just scraped my leg a little."

"It looks like it hurts." Brenda stares now, and I wonder if she can see the veins. It feels like they're quivering just beneath my skin, waiting to erupt. The entire surface of my body goes warm, and I wait for her to make another comment—to admit that the wriggling disgusts her as much as it disgusts me. I imagine that she'll take her unwieldy newbie needles and loop them under a vein and pull it out like a squirming tapeworm.

"You're making good time on it," Lettie says. "Might even finish with time to spare."

And then I hear Elmira's voice, whispering from the yarn stacks outside the classroom. "They'll come for you." I knit furiously, clicking my needles as loud as I can to block out the sound. The whisper echoes delicately around me every few minutes. It goes on for hours.

"Alright." Lettie pokes her head back into the room. "Closing time."

"Would you mind if I stay for a while?" I say. "I want to finish this section before I pack up. If you leave me your keys, I'll lock up and set the alarm before I go."

"Yeah, of course—but I can stay with you. Do some inventory or something. I don't want you to hang out all alone. It gets creepy in here at night by yourself."

I nod. "Sounds good."

Brenda and the others who've filtered in over the last several hours finish their rows and put their projects away. I continue to knit, listening to them chatter about meeting friends for drinks or husbands for dinner.

"I've heard scrubbing your hands with toothpaste works great to remove dye," Brenda says on her way out.

I nod. "Thanks—I'll give it a try." I haven't done anything at all to try to get the dye off—not when I'll be working on the blanket again the next day, anyway. And the day after that. Even the torn-up skin on my legs has started to turn blue from the transfer off my fingertips.

The shop descends into silence, save for Elmira's constant, quiet whispers. A few moments later, Lettie pauses by the door of the classroom. "I'm going to be doing some work up near the register. If you need anything, just holler. I'll come grab you when I'm ready to go, see how far you are to finishing your section."

I smile and nod. "Thank you." As soon as she's gone, I rip the bandage off my ankle and claw at my skin. A blue vein as thick as a crayon pops through. I gasp. I hike up my midi skirt to my thigh. The veins are everywhere and growing, pulsating in time to my fluttering heart. The revulsion comes in waves, drowning me deep in the horror of the roadmap cratering up across my right calf.

Just like in my dreams, my skin cracks, and the veins creep out. Elmira's laugh is mocking. I should be screaming, but a resolve is growing in me, too. I frantically search my bag for the gold scissors.

My stained fingers close over their sharp blades, and it's then I know what I must do.

I loop the tip of the scissors beneath the vein protruding from my ankle, then clip it loose. Tiny suckers shoot out, looking for something to anchor me to, but I zip the cutting edge of the blade up the vein length, all the way to the knee. A sheet of blood sprays my face, but it doesn't hurt. Not anymore. How could it? I clip the other end and pull loose the vein. It still heaves around as though fighting. These are Elmira's veins—they belong to her.

Now that I have a plan, it's easy. Zip, zip, zip, up one squiggling vein and down another. Snip the ends, pull them out. It's magical. With each vein squirming on the table, the heaviness leaves me. I am light as air. I am bright as stars. Lettie will forgive me the mess. I know she will—this blanket will be truly special. Unique. A tribute to Elmira the likes of which no one has ever seen.

I weave the vein ends into the blanket and pick up the strands along with Elmira's cashmere. The cables and the braid grow sticky with blood, and the knitted loops become gnarled—as gnarled as the veins had been in my legs. I knit with intensity, with purpose, slippery hands gripping the needles tightly.

Lettie's footsteps sound in the shop, coming nearer. Wait until she sees. Wait until they all see. "Quinn?" she calls. "What's that smell?"

My vision dims, and a different heaviness settles over me. Almost a peacefulness. A relief. I hold the blanket closer, admire my handiwork. It's both slick and gummy at once. My legs itch once more—I glance down, and this time I do scream. Another set of veins bursts up against my skin, inch by hideous inch, bulging through the jagged cuts. I lurch for the scissors. I'm snipping veins, fresh blood on my neck and spraying across the room, when Lettie finds me. Her face goes green, and she gags. Elmira laughs from behind her.

"God in heaven, what happened?" Lettie screeches. Her red page boy hair quivers.

I toss the scissors on the table and pop up from my chair. Thick, twisted veins hanging from my calves leak blood across the shiny tiled floor. "Look." I shake out the blanket. Drops go flying, landing in a spray on Lettie's arm. The twisted, gnarled weave sparkles red and blue in the light.

Lettie slumps, slow at first, and then suddenly, sprawling heavily to the floor. I crawl to next to her and arrange the blanket over us. I can barely keep my eyes open. All I need is a nap. Elmira nestles close and sings us a sweet lullaby. Just thirty minutes of sleep, and I'll be ready to knit the rest of these hideous veins into the last section of blanket.

NICOLE M. WOLVERTON is a Philadelphia, PA writer. Her short fiction has been previously published in magazines such as the Saturday Evening Post *and* The Molotov Cocktail*, as well as in anthologies from Dark Ink Books and Haunted MTL, among others. She is also the author of* The Trajectory of Dreams *(Bitingduck Press, 2013) and editor of* Bodies Full of Burning *(Sliced Up Press, 2021). Find her online at www.nicolewolverton.com and @nicolewolverton (Twitter).*

JULIE

Victoria Nations

Julie is that girl. She's the girl in the dorm hall, tousled and flushed. She's the girl with the backpack sliding off her shoulder, talking about a party that night, and the night after. And then it's Julie at the party, and Julie at the after party, and Julie at midnight, with a box of pizza at my dorm room door, and I open it to let her in.

Julie always brings the pizza. She weaves in and out of rooms down the dorm hall, offering slices and a wink. She lets in the pizza delivery guys and promises to introduce us to the cute one. Julie lets a delivery guy out of her room and passes out the pizza afterwards, giving grizzly details and laughing.

Julie is a freshman. Julie is a junior. Julie is a graduate student who is also the R.A., in a position of authority that gives her keys to all the dorm rooms. She's a transfer student from out of state. She's secretly married to a roommate we never see. Julie has lived her whole life in the dorm and seen generations of students come and go. Julie makes up stories, and they all involve pizza and us girls in the dorm. And we listen at her feet like acolytes, certain she's wise beyond our years.

She feeds us, pizza and stories.

But Julie eats her slices sitting cross-legged on her bed, watching through the open door, staring at us as we walk down the hall. And when she gestures for me to come in, I know she's chosen me.

Julie is beautiful. She has dark, sparkling eyes and dark, curling hair, and her lips are the deep red of marinara. Her skin is golden brown, sprinkled with moles, and flawless despite the pizza she constantly eats. She is blessed with curves that sway each time she moves down the hall. The dorm girls long for her ferocity and easy beauty, and I am captivated, too.

Julie is the best dorm mate because she doesn't care that we've gained the Freshman Fifteen or the Sophomore Twenty. She doesn't care if high school boyfriends have dumped us because of it. Julie roams the halls, pizza in hand, telling each girl she is beautiful in all the round, special places she has. Julie eats and beckons us to join her, and she calls us adorable even when sauce is smeared across our chins. She drags her finger and tastes it, and says we are delicious. She strolls out before we catch our breaths, singing that pizza is how she shows love.

Julie smells like warm yeast dough, and her scent fills the dorm. Hungry girls leave their rooms, following her. We are all driven a bit mad.

Julie stares and stops me outside her door. She watches my mouth as I try to speak. Her cheeks are flushed red when she pulls me into her room. We sit close on the bed, and she feeds me pizza, stretching the mozzarella with each bite until it snaps and hangs down my chin.

She leans in and bites the dangling cheese, tugging me into a kiss, then pulls me back against her, her legs wrapping around me in an embrace. She holds the pizza out again, and I lean back to take what she gives me.

I dream of her, that Julie sits astride me, offering pizza as delectable as she is. Bites of warm, melted cheese and sauce fill my mouth, and with each bite, she rocks forward. The bites come closer together. Julie feeds mouthfuls to me, leaning forward and holding my shoulder as she presses the pizza against my lips. Her hips press hard enough to make me gasp. Her hair hides her face in the dark, but her red lips are spread in a grin. She pulls the pizza away and takes her own bite, savouring it. Her groan of pleasure matches my own. I always wake up hungrier than before.

Dull-eyed girls drag down the halls, logy with midterms and carbs. Julie follows, picking up stragglers and prompting them to eat. They are growing plumper, and some worry about it. The girls pester me for diet tips while Julie hugs them, and they don’t notice when I don’t answer. Her eyes catch mine and it’s a gut punch. Hunger wracks me. Julie smiles at the pain on my face. She feeds me pizza when we’re alone, and I gobble it down, desperate to be filled. Julie teases that I’ll melt away, with my hollowed-out belly and breasts shrunk to nothing. I press my face into her soft body and knead her skin like dough in my hands. I fight the urge to take a bite.

Julie leaves pizza with me, and tells me to think of her, as if I could ever stop. Julie tells me it will be enough, that it will fatten me up and she’ll come back later. She tells me to eat it quick, but I wait, my mouth watering with anticipation. I smell Julie in the pizza, and see her in the toppings. And when I bite it, I taste her. I chew the cheese and feel the sauce burst between my teeth. Pleasure gushes through me, my head swimming with the sensations of pizza and Julie. She's everything in one slice of girl that I want, that I need.

Julie comes and I babble to her, trying to explain. She shushes me, delivery box in hand. I try to tell her, but she offers more pizza, and I am still so hungry.

Julie's room is cold in the morning. I've kicked the covers off, and I'm hardly awake when I realise I'm cowering in the corner. I'm squatting and chewing at my fingertips, holding a scream back that I thought I'd let out. The dark morning presses in around me, making me cower deeper, the metal bedpost jabbed into my side. Something was coming for me in a dream that my brain still tries to see.

I can't see anything in the dark.

Except for Julie. Her dark form lays curled under blankets, shallow breaths humming through the bed. My hands slowly unclench and I push back my tangled hair. They come away smeared with red. It surely is tomato sauce. I reach for her. I'm hungry again, and Julie will understand. She'll explain the sauce and drive the dream away. And we'll find more to eat.

The lump under the blankets doesn't move, but the breathing becomes ragged. I pull the covers off her, hoping she is waking up.

Sauce is soaked into the blankets and splattered across the sheets. My breathing hitches as I prod Julie again.

Julie is the girl who bounces into parties and lures me into her room in the hall. Julie is the girl with the plan and the pizza.

I lick the sauce from my fingers, and it tastes better than any I've ever had. Julie is covered in it. I lean down to kiss her and lick the sauce from her cheeks, her neck, and continue eating until I'm finally full.

VICTORIA NATIONS writes horror and gothic stories about creatures with emotional baggage. Her work appears in Gothic Blue Book, Volume 6, A Krampus Carol *and Burial Day Books' short fiction. She lives in Florida, USA with her wife and son, who indulge her love of monsters. Visit her online at LeavesandCobwebs.com and @Leaves_Cobwebs.*

CLIPPED WINGS

Emma Kathryn

Troubled men were my speciality and his anguish screamed through the realms. Foolishly, I thought I could save him. I had never seen one so temptingly disturbed and without hope. But I was up to the challenge, and he would be my greatest victory.

I came down from the heavens and stepped down on his ranch. The flesh on my back opened up to unleash my magnificent wings. I expected him to fall to his knees and submit to my brilliance. I didn't see the shovel before it was too late, and for the first time in my lengthy existence, I was knocked out cold.

I came to in a barn. Animal sounds and smells assaulted my senses as I roused. Sunlight danced through the rafters, but the heavy barn door was closed. I had to get out of here.

I flexed my wings, and they took up the entire breadth of the barn. Horses whinnied and pigs screeched. I pushed upwards, prepared to put a hole in the ceiling if I had to. I got less than six or seven feet up before I was yanked back down to the ground. Something grabbed at my ankles. Chains.

The barn door swung open, and I saw a silhouette. It was him, and he was holding a shotgun.

Seeing him up close shattered any illusions of a soul to be saved. His eyes were all hatred and hunger. He hadn't slept for months. I knew this because I had been watching him. A sense of foolishness bloomed within me.

"My Angel," he said, and tears welled in his eyes.

"You cannot keep me here," I told him.

"Beg to differ," he said, and tapped the shotgun against his leg.

"That can't kill me."

Bravado trumped his hesitation, and his hand cupped my cheek. Instinct kicked in, and I pressed my palm to his chest. That was all it took to send him flying across the barn, and into a stack of hay bales. Guilt shook me only briefly.

"And you can't kill a human," he cackled, dragging himself out of the hay. "I've done my research. You can't go home if I'm dead."

I'd never felt like this before. Composure drained away. Blind panic took over. I needed to go home. My wings unfurled to their fullest, and I tore the chains from where they held me down. Up, up, up I went…

The shotgun blast rang out. My entire world halted.

Then…

I…

Fell.

I hit the floor with a ringing in my ears and a burning like the fires of Hell in my left wing.

A smattering of holes of varying sizes marred my once magnificent white feathers. I wept uncontrollably.

"There you go," he snarled. "Won't be going anywhere now." Blood poured over the hay. "Clipping those wings works a hell of a lot better than chains, Angel."

Just when I thought he had done enough, something sharp and metal bit my neck. The world filled with blackness again.

When I woke, he was gone. My chains weren't, but were still attached to nothing on the other end. Just a pointless weight to drag around.

Agony flashed through me. My poor left wing was shattered. Even worse was the mess he'd made of my right side. He had actually attempted to clip my wings. What a sorry job he'd done of it. My body was a mess and it was all his doing.

For three days, I didn't move. Just curled up on my bed of hay and refused to answer his coos of "My Angel". He visited a few times a day. Usually to feed the animals, but sometimes just to stare at me and take pictures. He always brought that wretched shotgun.

On the fourth day, I waited until he was gone, and then I tried to fly. The failure of every fall and impotent flutter was disgusting. The exertion was unbearable and had probably done even more damage. I was never getting home now.

I retreated to my bed of hay for three more days. He came, he stared, he took more photographs of my broken wings.

On the seventh day, I accepted that my world was over. He walked into the barn with the shotgun, and I knew what I had to do.

As he whispered, “My Angel”, and leaned his dirty face over me, I did the unthinkable.

I took the shotgun and I blew his goddamned head off.

I was never going home, anyway. Nothing mattered but getting away from him.

I staggered from the barn, unlocking it with his blood-encrusted keys. Sun slapped my face, and I was stunned by how fresh the air was out here. The farmhouse was my only refuge. I considered hiding inside, but my clumsy, broken wings refused to let me in.

I couldn’t pull them into my shoulder blades to conceal them like before. They were stuck like this. Open and hideous.

Between my broken wings and my murder of a mortal, Heaven’s gates were closed to me forever. But I couldn’t find refuge among the mortals with these ghastly forms protruding from my back.

Farming tools lay scattered around the homestead. A scythe was propped against the wall of a small shed. It was sharp and would do the job.

Shearing my own wings was worse than killing my captor. Blood covered everything and I screamed the entire time. Once they were gone, I was just another mortal.

I made it into the house and called the number I had watched so many mortals in distress call. Emergency service workers decided I was a kidnap victim with no memory due to trauma. “Self-defence,” they all agreed. “No wonder, look at what he did to her.”

None of them questioned the white feathers drifting through the crime scene, and they didn't question the burnt-out remains of a pair of once-glorious wings in a trash can at the edge of the property.

EMMA KATHRYN is a horror fanatic from Glasgow, Scotland. You can find her on Twitter @girlofgotham. When she's not scaring herself to death, she is either podcasting as one half of The Yearbook Committee Podcast or she's streaming indie games on Twitch.

SKIN DEEP

Petina Strohmer

It was dark. It was cold. And she was naked.

That's all she knew for sure. The throb in her head was just the baseline to a symphony of pain playing throughout her whole body. A dull, persistent ache punctuated by excruciating high notes of spike, smart and sting.

Everything hurt.

She didn't dare move. Who knew what overtures of agony she'd start? Instead, she tried to concentrate, to think, to work out how she'd got here. Wherever the hell 'here' was. Her brain was too preoccupied with pain to remember and trying to force it just made everything worse.

Okay, she'd have to think *forward* instead—one small step at a time. Her heart was beating, her lungs were taking in air and she was conscious, although her internal chronometer knew that she had lost time. Her eyes were open, but she could see nothing. Was she blind, or blindfolded, or was there simply no light to see anything by? The way her eyes ached, this was probably a good thing, at least at the moment. Was she bleeding? Her face was stuck to the floor, but she'd had enough hangovers to know that may just be saliva. However, some of the ooze she could feel around her body was warm. That was not a good sign.

As her brain appeared to be still ‘offline’, she decided to ‘do’ rather than ‘think’—but very, very carefully. Her fingers twitched into life and she delicately ran them across as much of her body as she could reach. Strange bumps and ridges that she didn’t recognise were acutely tender to the touch. Returning her finger to her mouth, she tasted the metallic tang of blood. Was she bleeding out? If so, how long did she have to find help?

The floor was as smooth as it was cold. Tiles, perhaps, but even slowly stretching out her arms, she couldn’t feel any joins or edges. However, she did touch a vertical surface, possibly a wall, made of the same material. Very odd.

If she was inside somewhere, there had to be a door. As slowly as she could, she edged herself up onto her hands and knees. Her body screamed, her head swam, and as soon as she tried to inch forward, she was violently sick. The warm vomit splattered against the icy floor.

She wanted to scream and shout and cry but not only would that waste valuable energy but, in case there *was* anyone else here, it might not be safe. Biting back on the bitter bile, she pressed forward.

Finding that she couldn’t lean sideways across it, she worked out that she was in some kind of corridor. On and on she crawled until she met another wall, as cool and smooth as glass. A dead end.

There was nothing she could do now except rest and try to regain a little strength to drag herself back the way she came.

And so she sat.

Alone.

Afraid.

In agony.

Evie sat in front of the mirror, watching the tears roll down her face.

Jess put her hand on her friend's shoulder. "Don't do that, sweetheart." Evie didn't respond. "It's his fault, not yours," Jess tried again. "Spiteful bastard! That boy has an ugly soul."

"At least he can hide it." The words were no more than a whisper.

"Huh, obviously not well enough. Listen, normal people don't go around trying to hurt others, especially those who are obviously hurting enough already."

Turning away from the mirror, Evie ran her fingers down the red ridge on her cheek. "Perhaps I *do* look like Frankenstein's monster, all stitches and scars. "

"Oh, come on, you've been called much worse by much better than him."

Evie sighed. "Maybe, but I didn't love them."

"And you're going to be much better off when you don't love him anymore," Jess snorted. "You'll get over it, Hon. You've survived far worse." She took her friend's hand. "Anyone who can survive a car crash like that, then recover from injuries that the doctors said should have killed them, can walk tall. Evie, you've got this."

Evie turned back to the mirror. "Maybe I no longer want it." Again she traced the crooked, angry line that pulled down the skin of the eye at one end and puckered the lip-line at the other. There were worse scars criss-crossing her body; where the broken glass had cut, the fire had burned, and the rest of her was stitched and stapled back together. However, these were horrors that could be hidden, revealed only to someone she loved and trusted. Or thought she did. The rut down her cheek was impossible to mask. Make-up helped with the colour, but it couldn't disguise the asymmetry of her face. She knew, only too well, that people were acutely attuned to such things; it was a basic biological instinct to avoid individuals who appeared damaged or diseased.

"Have you heard anything more from the hospital?" Jess asked carefully.

Evie shook her head. "I'm still on the waiting list, but the list is just so long and every NHS emergency pushes me further down. I can't complain because I was one of those emergencies once and they pulled out all the stops to save me. Although," she bowed her head, "I'm beginning to wonder why."

Her friend leaned forward and hugged her, knowing that there were no simple answers to that one.

"How much?" Jess's eyes nearly fell out of her head, staring at the insurance settlement cheque.

Evie attempted a smile. "It's been a long time coming, and I'd rather the accident hadn't happened in the first place, but still…"

"True, but it *is* wonderful," Jess beamed. "Think of what you can do with that amount of money. Buy a house? Start your own business? The possibilities are endless."

"Well," Evie said decisively, "I know what I'm buying first."

"Are you sure about this?"

Evie nodded at her friend. "I've done my research, and it all seems legit. In fact, it has a stellar reputation—which is just as well considering how much it charges!"

The glossy leaflet indicated the quality of the clinic. The name "Visage" was printed on the bright blue sky above a photo of the state-of-the-art surgery. Inside, there were more shots of its gleaming facilities plus "before" and "after" photos, gushing testimonies and a biography of Dr Sven, a man obviously as well-qualified as he was handsome.

"Are you sure you're not going just to meet him?" Jess laughed.

"He's very nice," Evie told her. "Polite, professional—and just as gorgeous in the flesh."

"You've already been there?"

Evie nodded. "I'm booked in for next Thursday."

"Okay." Jess whistled through her teeth. "Do you want me to come with you?"

Evie laughed. "So you want a look at Dr Sven too, eh?"

The good doctor did not disappoint. He was tall and lean with sharp cheekbones and slender, well-manicured hands. His hair was a distinguished salt-and-pepper and the eyes beneath were bright blue. His Scandinavian accent just added to his overall appeal.

Evie could feel Jess smirking beside her and resisted the temptation to dig her in the ribs.

The doctor produced a picture with Evie's scarred face on one side and a computer graphic of how it would look after the surgery. "Of course," he smiled, "your face will take a little time to heal. I'm afraid you can expect some initial bruises, puffiness and a little soreness. However, when it has healed, you will look like your beautiful self again. In the meantime, I shall personally supervise your recovery."

This time, Jess's snort was almost audible. Evie kicked her foot.

Dr Sven stood, shadowing the two young women. "We shall see you on Thursday. If you have any questions in the meantime, be assured that I am fully available to you."

They waited until they were out of the door to giggle like schoolgirls. "Do you know what?" Jess sniggered, "I'm going to find something on my face that needs fixing if I can get that 'availability' too."

"Shut up!" Evie laughed. "Can you go and get the car? I've just got some papers to sign and the bill to pay."

Jess was suddenly serious. "You have to pay all that upfront? What if you're not satisfied with the result?"

"I will be." Evie smiled, producing her credit card.

"How do you feel?"

"It hurts a bit," Evie managed.

Dr Sven sat on the side of the bed. "We can up your pain relief if you like? Other than that, is everything all right?"

Evie nodded gingerly.

"The operation went really well," he told her. "I have released the tension on the eye and the lip and grafted healthy skin from your thigh over the scar itself." He dropped his voice. "You have such beautiful thighs, Evie."

She frowned, but the effects of the anaesthetic prevented her from coherent thought.

"Your friend Jess is outside." The doctor had reverted to his usual tone. "Would you like her to come in?"

"Please."

With armfuls of flowers and chocolate, Jess appeared in the doorway. "Are you okay?" she asked, bending to kiss the top of her friend's head gently.

"I think so," was all Evie could manage.

Holding the pre-op photo alongside her reflection in the mirror, Evie grinned.

"It's amazing," Jess agreed. "You're pretty much back to your old self—unfortunately."

Evie's eyes widened. "What do you mean?"

"Well, I'm never going to pull next to you in the clubs, am I? Back to playing second fiddle."

"Yeah, right," Evie laughed. She stretched out her neck and touched her chin. "I think I'll get rid of that too."

"What?"

"Well, a piece of glass cut into my chin during the accident. It was removed but it's left a mark."

"Show me." Jess peered at her friend's face. "Oh, it's like a cute little dimple. I'd keep that if I were you."

Evie frowned. "No, I think I'll have it done too."

Dr Sven was pleased. "Both of the procedures were a complete success. Your beauty is restored, lovely lady." He pulled some strands of hair away from her face, his fingers lingering just slightly over her repaired cheek.

"Er-erm, thank you." Evie felt a little uncomfortable without knowing why.

"What is this?" The doctor's tone cooled. He still held a lock of her hair and had pulled it back to reveal a tiny butterfly tattoo on Evie's neck.

"Oh, that. My mum loved butterflies, so I had a little one tattooed there in her honour."

"Hmmm." Dr Sven shook his head. "I'm not sure that a tattoo looks good on a beautiful young girl. I could remove it if you like?"

"No, no thank you," Evie faltered.

The doctor's bright blue stare bored into her. "So, what *shall* we do next?"

"I—I'm not sure what you mean."

A big, white smile. "Here at Visage we believe that perfection can always be improved upon." He reached out and gently pinched the bridge of her nose. "Did you get this in the accident?"

"Get what?"

"The bump in your nose."

"Oh no," Evie smiled. "I've always had that."

"But do you want it?"

She shrugged. "I've never really thought about it. It's just part of me."

"But do you want it?" he repeated. The stare had returned. "I hope you don't mind me saying but it does mar an otherwise very well-proportioned face."

"Have I got a big nose?" Evie asked casually over coffee.

"What's that you say, Beaky?" Jess laughed.

Evie didn't. "Have I, though?"

"Of course not. You've just been spending too long in the mirror lately."

Watching her reflection in the window, Evie touched the bridge of her nose. "It's got a definite bump here."

Jess finished her drink. “Think of it as a character feature.” When Evie didn’t reply, she added, “it’s fine, really. Don’t worry about it.”

“Where have you been?” Jess was irate. “I haven’t seen or heard from you for weeks. You’ve been ignoring my calls up until now. I was starting to get worried.”

“Sorry,” Evie said, down the phone. “I’ve just been snowed under at the office.”

“Right.” Jess was obviously unconvinced.

“Look, let me make it up to you. I’ll meet you at Costa’s at lunchtime and I’ll buy you a cake as compensation.”

Jess frowned. “You look… different.” Evie hid behind her coffee cup. “I can’t quite—wait—have you had your nose done?” Evie just smiled. “But-but why? I told you there was nothing wrong with it.”

“I decided otherwise.”

“*You* decided?” Jess narrowed her eyes.

“Yes, *I* decided.” Jess could hear the defensive tone in her friend’s voice. “Don’t you like it?”

“It’s fine. It’s all fine.” Jess’s mouth said one thing, but her tone said another. “Look, Jess, I’m told that plastic surgery is… addictive. Yes, you needed the first operation, maybe even the second. Just don’t get carried away. I know you fancy Dr Sven but—” Jess smiled.

Evie didn’t.

“Wow!” Evie pouted her freshly plumped lips. “They look great.”

Dr Sven smiled smoothly. "I told you. As I said, perfection can always be improved upon."

"But," Evie looked suddenly serious. "Jess will go mad when she sees them."

The doctor shook his head. "Jealousy is such a toxic emotion."

"I-I don't think she jealous," Evie said. "We've known each other forever. She's just worried—"

"That her friend is so much prettier than her."

"It's not—"

"Evie." Dr Sven closed his hand over hers. "I've been in this business a long time. Trust me, I know jealousy when I see it. Oh, please don't screw your beautiful face up like that. You'll only get frown lines and then we'll have to break out the Botox."

"Well, actually…" Evie began.

Jess rolled her eyes. "That man saw you coming. How much has he conned you out of so far?"

Evie was getting tired of hearing it. "*Actually*," she sniped, "the more treatments you have, the less each one costs."

Jessie banged down her cup. The other customers in the coffee shop stared. "Buy one, get one free should *not* apply to plastic surgery!"

"Keep your voice down," Evie hissed.

Instead, Jess produced her Costa loyalty card. "When you've got enough stamps, do you get a free boob job?"

"Shut up!"

“Why, are you embarrassed?” Jess replied loudly. “You should be.”

“Yes, I’m embarrassed.” Evie rose to her feet. “Of being seen with an ugly, jealous bitch like you!”

She slammed the door behind her.

“I tried to warn you.” Dr Sven’s dulcet tones oozed from Evie’s phone. “Please don’t upset yourself. Listen, let me take you to dinner this evening. Put the smile back on that pretty face.”

“Oh,” Evie faltered, “Is-is that ethical, doctor?”

“Relax Evie, it’s only dinner.”

She had never been to such an exclusive restaurant. Crystal chandeliers, silk tablecloths, and a string quartet. Evie stopped in the doorway. “Oh, I-I’m not—”

Dr Sven placed a hand on the middle of her back. “Like a precious diamond, a beautiful lady deserves a beautiful setting.”

As they walked to their table, Evie noticed several elegant women smile at the doctor. “Are they your clients?” she asked them.

“Now, *that*, I really cannot say,” he whispered, returning their greetings.

What Evie didn’t see was the knowing looks those women shared with each other as they passed.

The wine and conversation flowed until Evie stopped noticing how often the doctor touched her; on the hand, the arm, the neck, the knees, the thighs.

"I'm sorry about Jess," he said, then smiled. "But I bet the boys appreciate your new look." Evie laughed and shook her head. "No?" the doctor theatrically, "Even your boyfriend hasn't noticed?"

"I don't have a boyfriend," she told him.

He leaned in close to her ear and whispered, "Interesting."

She was drunk—but not *that* drunk.

"No," Evie said, trying to remove Sven's hand from her thigh in the back of the taxi.

His hold remained firm. "Oh, come on," he cooed. "Don't be ungrateful. I have brought out the true beauty in you and beautiful people should be… together."

"You're my doctor," she protested.

His hand slid up further. "No, I am your alchemist," he muttered. "You owe your beauty to me."

"What?"

Sven's lips grazed her cheek. "I am in love with you."

Evie shook some sense into her head. "What are you talking about? You don't love me, you don't even know me. All the great Dr Sven is in love with is his own handiwork!"

He tried to silence her by closing his mouth over hers.

She pulled away. "Stop it!"

The driver pulled his cab to the kerb, then leaned around in his seat. "You okay, luv? Do you need help?"

The doctor removed his hand and bowed his head. "I'm sorry," he said, "too much champagne. I'm terribly sorry, Evie. Please forgive me."

Warm with wine herself, Evie eventually nodded. "Okay."

The cabbie was still looking at her. "Everything all right?"

She nodded.

"Sure?"

She nodded again, and the cabbie resumed the drive.

His passengers sat in silence for the rest of the journey. When they arrived at Evie's place, Sven took her hand. "Thank you for tonight—and for accepting my apology. To show my gratitude, there will be no charge for your next procedure."

It took her intoxicated brain a moment to process this. She frowned. "What next procedure?"

He threw open his hands. "What would you like?"

Evie's phone beeped again. She squinted at it in the morning light. Five missed calls and fifteen unread messages—all from Jess. "Huh," Evie muttered. "You can stew in your own juice, madam."

She climbed out of bed and made her way into the bathroom. Examining her face in the mirror, she was happy with what she saw. A few months ago, she thought she'd never want to see her reflection again. Sven may have misbehaved last night, but he did apologise sincerely and, she thought, touching her unblemished cheek, his work *was* perfect.

Her phone beeped again. Another message from Jess. *I'm worried about you. We need to talk. Please call me.*

Evie ignored it and began her morning ablutions. The phone rang. "Seriously?" She picked it up, expecting to cut off the call, but it wasn't Jess.

"Good morning." Dr Sven's voice lilted down the line. "Did you sleep well?"

"Like a log. And you?"

"Oh, I'm up and in work already. I'm looking at my diary. When would you like to come in?"

Evie's hungover head didn't understand. "Come in?"

"For your next procedure."

"I—"

"It's free, remember."

"Oh, you really don't need to do that. It's not—"

"Oh, but I really do. I behaved very badly yesterday and I need to make it up to you, Evie."

She had another look at her reflection. "I don't think I need anything else done, actually."

"Perfection can—"

"Always be improved upon," she finished for him.

"Of course."

"Look, give me a little time to think about this and I'll get back to you." There was no reply. "Dr Sven?"

"Okay." That cool, more measured tone of voice again. "Don't leave it too long, please."

And then he was gone.

There was a knock at the door. Evie frowned. “Can’t I get over this hangover in peace?” She looked through the peephole to see Jess’s distorted face. With a sigh, she opened the door.

“Oh Evie, thank God,” Jess began.

“What do you want?”

“Er—can I come in?”

“What do you want?” Evie repeated coldly.

“I need to talk to you.”

“About?”

“Dr Sven.”

“Goodbye.” Evie closed the door.

But Jess wasn’t easily deterred. “Evie, I did some digging and had a good look into this man.” No reply. “When you peel back the glossy veneer—”

“Go away, Jess.”

“There are rumours—lots of them. To do with some of the women he’s treated. Something’s not—”

But Evie was now in the shower and couldn’t hear a word.

“Hello, beautiful lady.” Dr Sven was all smiles again as Evie was shown into his office. “Have you made up your mind?”

Evie couldn’t help but return the smile. “Actually, I have.” She pulled down her neckline to reveal a large mole at the top of her breast.

"I've had it since birth," she explained, "and it's never given me a cause for concern. In fact, I used to call it my Nell Gwyn beauty spot."

The doctor laughed.

"But, on reflection," Evie continued, "it *is* a bit big and you can never be too careful with these things."

"Very true." The doctor nodded.

"So, I'd like it removed, please."

"That's a simple enough procedure," the doctor told her, "which I can fit in this afternoon if you're free."

"Really?" Evie was surprised.

"Are you free?"

"Er—erm—I can be."

"I'll see you at three."

When Evie arrived back home, there was a note waiting for her on the hall mat. She recognised Jess's handwriting but started to read it anyway.

Evie, please don't ignore me. This is important. I know you like Dr Sven and what he is doing for you but—

Evie screwed the note up and threw it in the bin.

"Ready?"

"As I'll ever be."

"Well," Dr Sven said, "this is not your first procedure, so I guess you know what to expect."

"I should do."

"Yes, you should." He produced a syringe. "I shall anaesthetise the area now and very soon, it will all be over."

She shivered in the cold darkness. Rubbing her arms to keep herself warm had proved too painful.

Suddenly the place was filled with searing light. She screwed her face up against the pain as the bright barbs stabbed her eyes.

There was still no sound so as carefully as she could, shading her face with her hand, she tried to take a peek. She was greeted by blazing blades that sheared through her brain. Feeling that she would be sick again, she jammed her hand over her eyes.

As quickly as the light came on, it went off again. She removed her hand and was immediately blinded by a second brilliant flare.

Feeling that she was already disorientated enough, the best option seemed to be to wait and see whether there was a pattern to this. After a while, it appeared that the illumination was stuttering on and off as if the bulbs were faulty or a connection somewhere was loose. Although there was no definite rhythm to it, she thought that if she kept her hands close to her eyes, she might be able to catch a glimpse of her strange surroundings. Steadying herself against the polished wall, she rose to her feet and waited for another flare. When it came, she opened her eyes.

A figure flashed in front of her.

It was only briefly, but now she knew she wasn't alone. Friend or foe, she had to try to talk to them. Her voice cracked in her throat. "Hello?"

No reply.

"Hello?" she tried again.

Still nothing. The person had appeared close by, but despite straining her ears, there was no noise.

"Who are you? What's going on here?"

The darkness swallowed the sound. She shielded her eyes and waited for the next flash of light.

When it came, it lasted long enough for her to learn that the figure was female—and in a very sorry state. She hadn't been able to distinguish much detail, but there was a lot of blood.

"Are you okay?" she called into the gloom. It hurt to talk, but she needed to know what was happening. Still receiving no reply, she stretched out her arms and stepped forward. One, two, three paces and her fingertips touched another cold wall. Where had the girl gone?

Another burst of illumination, lasting a little longer this time. The figure had returned. Her body was battered and bruised, and she was covered in vivid lacerations that were bleeding profusely. Tears ran from eyes that were no more than dark slits, running with the blood from a shattered nose and a split lip.

She stared, in a state of shock. The hideous figure had opened its mouth in a silent scream, revealing a swollen purple tongue and several broken or missing teeth. It reached out its arms and everything went black. She scrabbled around in the darkness for the body but, once again, it had disappeared.

What the hell was going on here? Who was the girl? How did she get into that state? Had she been brutally assaulted and left to bleed out? And, if so, by whom? And why?

And was the same going to happen to *her*?

Feeling light-headed, she leaned back against the wall. Lifting her hands to her face, she found it was both wet and very sore, although her mouth was numb. Had she already been beaten? It felt like it. However, looking at the other girl, she thought she'd got off lightly. Or was there more to come?

She waited for the next flare, hoping for some answers. Nothing happened for the next few minutes while she stewed. There was still no sound from the girl, but she was sure she could hear something…

Something grabbed hold of her from behind. She screamed.

The light suddenly glared, revealing someone at her back. It wasn't the girl, but taller, with an unblemished face.

It spoke. "Do you like what you see, Evie?"

She recognised that accent immediately and turned to face him, but he grabbed her head and twisted it back to the front. "Why not take a closer look?"

Dr Sven shoved her forward, and she put out her hands to stop herself colliding with the grotesque girl. Her flattened palms hit the opposite wall.

She shook her head in confusion. The girl shook her head back.

"What's going on?" Evie mouthed, feeling the blood running down her chin.

"It's probably just the anaesthetic wearing off," the doctor told her. He moved in closer behind her. "Isn't she pretty?"

"What have you done to her?" Evie tried again.

"Oh, lots of things." Sven laughed. "And then I undid them all again."

"Why?"

"God giveth and God taketh away," he said simply, "especially from ungrateful little girls."

Evie was starting to feel faint. "I-I don't know—"

"Those who do not honour the creator of their beauty. It's blasphemy."

"She did that?"

"Oh yes, 'she' did." Sven's voice was tinged with anger.

"Who is she?"

He put his hand behind Evie's head and pushed her nose into the glassy wall. "You really don't recognise her?" He brushed the matted hair away from her shoulder to reveal a small butterfly tattoo.

Evie stared at her reflection in the mirrored wall.

"Oh my God!" She staggered backwards. "What have you done to me?"

Sven shrugged. "Taught you some manners?"

Evie stared down at her mutilated body. Deep gashes had been loosely resewn like a grisly jigsaw puzzle. Blood seeped from everywhere and trickled down her legs onto the mirrored floor. Tears ran from her puffy eyes.

"We always end up hurting the ones we love." Sven shook his head. "It's going to leave some serious scars, I'm afraid." He lowered his mouth to her ear. "Maybe we can fix them when you learn to be more… grateful."

Evie turned and tried to get away, but in every direction she ran into more mirrored walls. Sven laughed as she repeatedly staggered and fell. "You can run," he called, "but you definitely can't hide, not in this place. You're too small, soft and slippery to do much damage to the mirrors. Nor can you escape. I built this maze and only I know how to get out of it."

But Evie kept trying. Slipping on the wet, red floor, she charged at every mirror in a vain attempt to find which one was a door. Soon they were all smeared with blood, and she was exhausted. She sank into a sobbing heap on the floor.

"Finished?" the doctor asked as he strolled towards her. "It usually takes the feisty ones a while to realise that there is no way out."

The feisty *ones*?

Who else was in here, had been here, or would be here? Fuelled by anger, Evie felt some of her strength return. She hadn't gone through everything in her life without building some serious mettle. She wasn't stupid, either. The mirror behind Sven revealed the big metal boss of his keyring poking out of his back pocket.

Assuming the appearance of defeat, she rose slowly to her feet and held out her hands. "Okay," she said, "you win. I admit I've been a spoilt little bitch and I should have shown more… gratitude. I mean, how hard is it to return the love of such a brilliant man?"

Sven smiled. "You're learning."

"I am." She walked towards him with a semblance of a smile. "You know, when I first met you, Doctor, I was really bowled over."

"Well—"

With the full force of her desperation and rage, Evie launched herself forward and sent Sven crashing into the mirror behind him. The boss of his keyring hit the shiny surface hard, and the glass shattered into sharp shards. She grabbed one and held it out in front of her.

The two of them stared at each other like a couple of cats.

Suddenly, he reached for a shard of his own, but she had anticipated this and stabbed his hand. He stared at the scarlet slash, dropping his own blood onto the glassy floor. "Try that again, Doctor," she warned him, "and I'll take your eyes out."

He tilted his head, then smiled. "Clever girl. Are you going to give me a taste of my own medicine?"

"Or slit your throat," she growled.

"You could," he agreed, "but then you'd never find your way out of here. Hmmm…" He put his finger to his chin. "Will you die of dehydration or blood loss first, I wonder?"

Feeling the life already draining out of her, Evie knew she must stay focused. If she lost consciousness now, she could die. Either that or she could spend who-the-hell-knew-how-long trapped and tortured in this madman's mirrored maze. She already knew that there were much worse things in life than death.

"Well, since I'm in charge now," Evie told the doctor, "how about I run through some options?" For a moment, she revelled in the power of control. She could see how he had become addicted to this. "Let's see. You can dump me at the nearest hospital where they may, or may not, be able to stop me bleeding to death. However, as you well know, I am a survivor. Even if you make your getaway, you'll have to spend the rest of your life in obscurity." She smiled. "That would be the cruellest torture for a man of your ego. And, as if that wasn't enough, you'd better keep one eye over your shoulder at all times too because I *will* be coming for you."

"Or?"

"Or, *I* cut *you* to ribbons, right here, right now. I already know what an excruciating way to die that is. If, as you say, you always hurt the ones you love, imagine what I can do to someone I despise. Then, when I'm done…" She pointed the glass dagger at her own throat. "I probably won't even feel it now so it will be a quick, easy end for me."

Sven stared at her. "You wouldn't."

"Wouldn't I?" Evie opened her arms. "Look at me." She crouched down in front of him, the glass still in her hand. "I said, look at me!"

She stared into his eyes. Without control, he was a lost soul. She had him now.

"Look at my body. Look at this face. Oh, doctor, you should never leave your enemy with nothing to lose."

She held the sharp silver sliver up in front of him. "So, Sven, what's it going to be?"

Originally from London, PETINA STROHMER now lives in Wales, UK. Her first novel, Truly Blue; A Rock & Roll Parable, *was published by Leaf Books in March 2009. Her second novel,* Entertaining Angels, *was published by Cinnamon Press in May 2016. She also writes award-winning short stories, plays and magazine articles. For more information, go to www.petinastrohmer.com.*

DODO TI PITIT MANMAN

Michelle Mellon

She held the dustpan at arm's length and gagged a bit as she watched the oversized insect carcasses slide into the garbage can. Too anxious to get any closer, she banged the lid shut using the dustpan. Then, when she couldn't stop shivering, she took a long, late-afternoon shower.

That night, lying in bed, it all seemed rather silly. Given the number and size of the creatures, could they have been a child's toys? Slid under the old stove who knew how long ago, in a game that ended in tears when the bugs were lost for good?

She hadn't looked too closely. Hadn't wanted to, really. There was just enough time to sweep the debris into a pile off to one side and toe a damp paper towel across the grunge adhering to the vinyl floor before the deliverymen came back in bearing her new stove.

Now, alone in what seemed an oversized bed in an oversized house, she thought about those oversized things and decided they must have been realistic-looking rubber toys. Although why anyone would want their child to play with something that looked so terrifying was beyond her. Like a mutant cross between an ant and a spider. She couldn't imagine.

Except, of course, that she could. And she did. Until she stopped trying to fight the urge and got up and poured herself a glass of wine.

Just a temporary ritual, she'd told herself in those early days after he'd left her. It was a way to wash away the day and soothe herself before preparing dinner for one. But the stove delivery had upset her schedule and after the shower she'd had leftovers and forgotten and now she couldn't get it out of her head—any of it—so she needed that glass of wine.

After two glasses she was finally able to drift off, the ugly creatures slipping from her mind. And she started to dream about more pleasant things. Like a walk through a meadow of flowers. But after a while in the heat of the sun, with the scent of the flowers and the pollen and grabbing tendrils of grass of the meadow, she was starting to itch.

She swiped at her forehead. Rubbed her arms against her sides, hoping to not have to scratch her armpits. Even the back of her knees felt slick and uncomfortably crawly. She scratched and slapped, and her fingers came away with the sense of bumping over tiny moving objects.

No longer moving now. She looked down and her long fingernails had scrapings of bug carapaces with soft insides. She wanted to scream and strip down and wipe herself free of the invading insects. Instead, she flailed and whimpered and fell into a deeper sleep.

It took a while to make sense of the prickling sensation. Like tiny probing touches to test the landscape. Then a small suckling, like a baby at a breast. Like the ghost of the baby she never had. Would never have. Would never watch grow into a toddler that would slide their oversized creepy toys under the range for some unsuspecting soul to find many years later.

Maybe not a baby, then. Something else. She swatted, as if *he* would be there, probing with teeth and tongue, trying to get her into the mood. Baby-making, he called it. But when they found out there'd be no babies of their own, he'd left her.

Her hand only hit air and flopped onto an empty pillow above an empty side of a lonely bed. Story of her life. She'd thought about adopting a child on her own, providing the kind of forever home she'd never had growing up. She had a stable, work-from-home job making good money. The house was in her name, and she lived in a multicultural neighbourhood near a top-ranked charter school. But she hadn't made the leap.

She probably wouldn't have made a good mother, anyway. Her own had abandoned her. Just walked out, leaving her in a box on a random doorstep in the middle of the night with no note. Was it something you learned, mothering? Or was it something instinctual—something you were born with?

The tugging sensations hadn't gone away, and she realised she was awake. She still hadn't exchanged the filmy night things he liked for practical flannel things she could roll out of bed and continue the day in. So, as she pulled the covers away, she could easily see the bulge of her nipples and small shadowed shapes causing the semi-sheer nightgown to ripple.

She felt a tightening in her breasts, a swelling. She had a moment of joy when she thought they'd awakened and were ready to nourish. Maybe she wasn't fully awake; perhaps she was dreaming she had given birth and was ready to feed a child. Then she felt the pinching and sting of miniature mouths and realised she was having an allergic reaction to the creatures biting her.

She clawed at her tingling breasts and pulled the flimsy gown away from her body in different directions until it tore along the seams. As she tossed the remnants aside, she could see an undulating mass of black shiny bodies atop her brown skin. The moonlight gave the scene a mystical hue, as if she weren't watching the ruin of her own self.

Like her chocolate aureoles bubbling up with blisters that enveloped the bugs that caused them. Or watching the flat brown stomach for which she prided herself move in uneven waves, insects riding the distended folds of skin so taut it was splitting and softening back down under rivulets of escaping pus. Or feeling her thighs, so large and strong now swollen into timbers of tenderised flesh so sensitive that each multi-legged step upon them felt like the snide dart of a stealthy tattooist's needle.

She could fight. She always had before. There was always one more adventure waiting around the corner. One more thing to learn and see and do. Even when he had become her everything, he hadn't squelched that inside her. But she didn't feel strong anymore. Or, more accurately, she didn't feel like fighting. When was it her time? When would it ever be her time just to rest?

She could no longer feel the nips and pinches. She no longer cared if they were real or a product of her imagination. She embraced the numbness willingly, lovingly, and let it carry her where it would.

"And plenty of rest," were the last words the doctor said as the ambulance doors closed.

She was going home. It had been weeks of recovery and relapse and recovery and therapy, but she was finally going home. They sent her in an ambulance as a precaution because she was still so fragile, and as the attendants gently settled her into her guest room, she breathed a sigh of relief. (Even with the house fumigation and removal of her old bedroom furniture she couldn't stomach the thought of returning to that room quite yet.)

"It's okay, dear, they're gone. It's just you and me, now."

She started at the sound of the home nurse's voice. The overhead light was off and the curtains were drawn, so in the feeble late afternoon light the other woman was little more than a silhouette in the doorway.

"Drink some water," the shadow urged, indicating a glass on a coaster on the bedside table. "You need to keep up your strength."

She took a sip, then gulped the rest and could have easily downed three more glassfuls.

"That's it," the nurse crooned. Even as she slipped closer, the light through the windows did nothing to illuminate her features. In fact, things looked darker and more out of focus by the second.

"…something… help you… sleep now…"

Someone was holding her hand and singing softly. "*Dodo ti'pitit manman, Dodo ti'pitit papa, Si vlé pa dodo crab la va manger…*"

The song was familiar. It reminded her of the Haitian grandmother she'd met a few times as a child, but she couldn't remember what all of the words meant. Something about sleep and a baby-eating crab?

Her mind was tired and unfocused. Someone was speaking. The nurse. She was the one who had been holding her hand and crooning. But the things she was saying didn't make any more sense than the lullaby.

"I'm here for you. I was here when it started, and I'm still here."

"Wha—?"

"I knew what I had to do when I saw them taking away that old stove. That's where they hid, you know?" The nurse's gaze lifted, and she stared at a dark spot on the wall as she talked.

"She was always fascinated by bugs. So, I got her those toys. And she told me they talked to her, but I didn't believe her. Even though she'd never lied to me before. She always told me everything!" she exclaimed, her eyes darting back down briefly to make contact before glazing over again.

"Like how they told her if she sent those play bugs to the dark and secret places where the real bugs lived, they'd play with her, and share dark and secret things with her."

"Who—?"

"I couldn't save her; I didn't know how." The nurse pressed on. "But I went back to school and I learned. Now, with you, I have a second chance. I've been waiting a long time. All those renters in that house after we moved out. Too temporary. Then you bought it and I waited."

"For wha—?"

"I kept those killers when we moved out, you see? Collected them, contained them, cared for them and their children and their children's children. My husband left, but I moved in across the way and I waited. And that day when I saw them take away that old stove, I slipped those bugs inside the house to see if it was just the stove and just my girl they had been greedy for or if they'd try to take you, too."

"You… did this?"

"No, honey, you're not listening. It was them. They did try, didn't they?" The nurse whistled, half in admiration. "My daughter was so unrecognisable. So small, yet so unnaturally large. But you, well of course you're bigger. Not much bigger, petite as you are. But stronger."

The woman on the bed made a noise somewhere between a chuckle and a snort of derision. She felt nowhere in the neighbourhood of strong.

"Yes, they did a number on you. I couldn't quite see from across the way, of course, but after I called 911 and told them I heard screaming coming from your place, I raced to the hospital for my shift so I could be there for you."

The woman's eyes were wide as the pieces of the nurse's story assembled themselves in her muddled mind.

"Now don't worry, dear, you didn't scream loud enough that I could hear you. But you should have, judging by the look of you. When they wheeled you into the ER even the old hands were gasping. I mean, you were such a sight!

"Of course, you don't remember, and thankfully so. But your cheeks had swollen so much that only the tiniest buds of your lips remained. And your nose was just an impression in a landscape of overflowing flesh. It's a miracle you could still breathe."

The nurse nodded emphatically and took a deep breath of her own. "We wouldn't have known where your eyes were without those lovely big brows of yours. It was almost like we were looking at an oversized jug instead of your head, with those two tiny ears sticking out like undersized handles."

The nurse laughed as if she were relaying a delightful memory they both shared.

"Your body, though. Your teeny tiny frame supporting all that bulk. You looked about ready to burst. Your torso and limbs were a single swollen mass. Everything looked painfully tight, like an overstuffed sausage with the casing so thin you could see everything moving underneath. The vessels and… other things. Things they left behind."

The nurse shuddered, but her eyes gleamed as she continued.

"And there were thin trails of blood that disappeared into valleys of flesh and spilled over inflamed hillocks like small waterfalls."

The woman on the bed moaned at the poetic recitation and tried to turn away. She felt like the subject of a biblical verse or a cautionary tale. But her will was quicker than her muscles. Everything felt slow and heavy and terrible.

"You were puffed up so big, then. Now you're so shrunken and small."

The nurse proved her point by leaning over the bed and holding up a hand mirror. Her patient looked in horror at the twisted, scarred flesh staring back at her. She was an oversized walnut; an unrecognisable wrinkled patchwork of human parts writhing in mental anguish while the nurse nattered on.

"…second chance. Like my own helpless child. I'm going to take care of you and never leave you alone again for the monsters to have."

The woman screamed. Fear, anger, frustration. Tears rolled down the marred plains of her face, and she wondered that the world didn't come running as she cried out. But the damage to her skin restricted the opening of her mouth, and some of the parasites she'd hosted had damaged her lung capacity. The scream she heard in her head was, in reality, only a high-pitched groan.

The nurse filled the water glass from a pitcher and added a few drops of something from a vial in her pocket. "You drink this up and calm yourself now," she soothed.

Through her tears, she glared at the glass and the nurse. There was fight in her; there would always be fight in her. But as she lifted a shrivelled hand off the bed comforter, she wondered now what she was fighting for.

Her hand wavered toward the glass. Then she got a solid grip and, giving herself up to fate once again, chugged the water and began to drift off to sleep. Next to her, the nurse settled in, wiping the other woman's prematurely furrowed brow and stroking her moist, contorted cheek while singing softly.

"*Dodo ti'pitit manman…*"

MICHELLE MELLON has been published in more than two dozen speculative fiction anthologies and magazines and is a member of the Horror Writers Association and the Science Fiction and Fantasy Writers Association. Her first story collection was published in 2018. For updates on her work, visit www.mpmellon.com and/or follow her on Twitter: @mpmellon.

WRITTEN ON HER SKIN

Nico Bell

There was no time to grab a jacket. If she wanted to survive the fire, she had to escape her burning apartment building in only her pyjamas—shorts and a tank top.

"Everyone out!"

She recognised the voice of the old man—the one who lived next door and did her grocery shopping, leaving two paper bags full of essentials in front of her door every week so she didn't have to venture down the crowded streets to the store around the corner. He shouted the warning as his footsteps pounded down the hallway.

It'd been eight months since she'd left her building, but she couldn't let that stop her.

She swung open the door and took off running. Her bare feet thumped in unison with the others filling the crowded space as they shuffled down the stairwell and busted out into the chilly city night.

"Holy crap." The old man stood off to the side, staring up at the building which was quickly becoming engulfed by flames. "What are we going to do now?"

Her skin started to itch as the street filled with onlookers, each mumbling or chattering or murmuring to each other, pointing first to the flames, and then to the poor occupants now out on the street in nothing but their pyjamas.

A stranger stared directly at her. His eyes grazed down her curvy body, taking in her small breasts and round hips, pausing briefly to examine her ass before allowing his eyes to tour her smooth legs. From her spot on the street, she couldn't make out the word he uttered as his lips parted. It didn't matter that his sound got lost in the nip of winter between them, as her home burned to ash, because as she shivered, a familiar flick of pain etched beneath her skin, and she knew with certainly the name he'd called her.

And she knew, without looking at her leg, that the name surfaced on her calf, freshly carved in her own blood, for the world to see.

Panic rose in her chest. She needed to get off the street and find someplace safe immediately.

Rosemary's apartment. Yes, that was only a few blocks away. Her old co-worker had always been kind, always said, "If there's ever anything I can do for you." The sweet woman had once hosted a poker night where they gossiped in the corner drinking beers while the other co-workers played cards. Yes, Rosemary would open her door. After all, this was an emergency.

She pushed past the gawkers. Her feet picked up speed as more distance separated her from the fire. Sirens wailed in the distance, and she took off running at full speed.

If you have to be outside, move as fast as possible to find a safe place.

Her mother's words of wisdom echoed in her mind as she hurried. The city buzzed with late night activity. People loitered outside of bars, smoking and laughing, and one man saw her coming, barrelling down the street, and blocked her path. She was going to dip around him, but he blocked her way, and she skidded to a stop, almost running into him.

"Whoa, what's the hurry, sweetie?"

It felt like a knife under her skin, writing each letter with precision and care. This time, it showed up on her thigh. Small, but deep and red.

Sweetie. It was now a part of her.

He was too drunk to notice. "You look cold. How about I buy you a drink and warm you up?"

A car honked and distracted him, giving her an opening to escape. She started running.

"Hey! Where you going?"

She sped up, as if she could outrun what she knew was coming next. But it didn't work like that, and she forced herself to keep going against the searing heat of a new word starting to carve on her other arm. A word he hurled at her for having the audacity to leave him on the street, to not engage with him.

B-I-T-C-H.

The buildings shook her old memories of walking to Rosemary's place, back before her condition started. There was nothing unusual that caused it to begin. There didn't need to be some great big catalyst, at least that's what her mom said over the phone that first night. The words appear and eventually fade, but the condition lasts.

Forever.

"Baby, why you running?" A man sitting on a building's front steps called out to her and followed it up by whistling at her.

Her calf burned as the careless name he'd called out became a part of her skin.

"Whoa, Angel. How about you run over here and give me your number?" Another man, another name, another wave of pain as it sliced itself into her neck.

It'd been so long since she'd run, and the cold air tightened her lungs as her bare feet began to slow. Her side hurt as she sucked in air and pushed herself to keep going.

More people. More names came barrelling at her.

"Hey, sexy."

"Looking good, sweetheart."

"Want some dick, whore?"

Each word rose to the surface of her flesh and pressed forward, marking her for everyone to see. Tears clouded her vision, but she spotted Rosemary's building just one more block away. She forced herself to keep moving.

A man driving a car slowed and rolled down his window. "Hey slut, show me those titties!"

She couldn't take it. Her legs gave out, and she crumbled to the pavement as S-L-U-T etched into her forehead.

"Oh my God, are you okay?" A man approached and leaned down. He gasped as he read over the words. "What happened to you? Do you need me to call an ambulance?"

She laid on her back and let the tears slide down her cheeks.

"Whoa, what's up with her?" A stranger walked past, looking down in disdain.

"She's probably a drunk or a junkie," another replied, and leaned down to get a better look. "Shit, look at her skin. She probably did it to herself. Fucking psycho."

"Does she need help?" another person asked, already getting out their phone, already pressing the button to take a picture before calling 911.

"Ugh, pathetic."

"What a loser."

"Slut. Who goes out in this weather wearing next to nothing?"

"Probably just some bitch detoxing."

She wanted to scream out, to beg them to stop talking, to keep their words to themselves, but the pain of each new letter on top of each new letter on top of each new letter caused her cry to get stuck in her throat.

The black sky stared down at her. Somewhere, behind the lights and smog and clouds, there were stars.

Beautiful shiny stars.

She tilted her head to the side and looked through the sea of legs and people who had gathered, and she spotted the steps to Rosemary's apartment.

She'd almost made it.

Almost.

NICO BELL is the author of horror novella Food Fright *and the editor of horror anthology* Shiver. *She's had several short stories published in both horror and romance. She can be found at www.nicobellfiction.com and on Twitter and Instagram @nicobellfiction.*

A ROTTEN THING

Nicola Kapron

Hello again, my darling. It's been a while, hasn't it? Long enough that I'm afraid I've forgotten your name. Please don't take offense, my sweet. I've forgotten my name as well. Our children's faces have blurred into smears of tan skin and dark hair in my mind's eye. Their voices, though—their voices linger. I can still hear the sobbing. The stifled screams. A thousand little noises that ran down my spine like needles. I didn't know a sound could stab through flesh like a knife before I met you.

There are no children in our house now. My sweet little spores were taken away. Nothing is left but rotting wood, dust-filled insulation, and damp, dark earth. Nothing grows here but me. And you, of course. How could I forget about you?

Did you know that fairy rings are the remains of old trees? The fungus grows in circles to mark the graves of ancient stumps. No wonder there are so many stories about the fair folk, the good neighbours, the kindly ones, getting royally pissed off when people disrespect those mushroom circles. If some big, clumsy bastard carelessly stepped into my grave, I'd be pissed off, too. Even if it was you. Especially if it was you.

We were happy. Nobody ever believed me when I told them so, but we were: you, with your big, calloused hands, your breath reeking of beer, your eyes red, raw, and aching. Me, with my necklace of fading green bruises and purple running down my thighs like stockings. I chose you, over and over, because you always seemed like the better option. Breaking my wings to stay cramped and quiet in the house of my parents, or you. Trying to make it alone by waiting tables and working corners, or you. Running helpless into the streets with two small children, no education, and no skills, or you. When you put it like that, it's no wonder I picked you every time.

But it's not like it was all bad, right? It can't have been. If you were only ever awful, I wouldn't have stayed. So let's talk about the happy things: bouquets of wildflowers, sloppy kisses, the strength of your solid arms around me. Quiet moments, peaceful moments, moments where I wasn't making your knuckles go white. They existed, I'm sure. We were happy together. What's one night of blood and pain compared to that? Broken glass in my feet, the bones of broken nose sliding back into my brain? It was an honest mistake, my dear—you told me so, weeping, as you drove me out into the woods and started to dig. We all make mistakes. I've been dead long enough to let this one go.

Does that mean I've forgiven you? Well, sort of. It means I've accepted what you did, and I've come to understand why. I still don't agree with your actions, of course, but it's a bit late to change anything there. You have to live with what you've done, and I—we'll come back to me later. Let's talk about you, first.

I still remember the taste of dirt in my mouth. The wet snap of bone as you forced my stiff limbs into the hole. Digging a grave is so much harder than they make it look on TV, isn't it? When the deed was done, you drove back home and parked in the driveway. I drifted after you, like spores on the wind. You stayed out there all night, head in your hands, apologising to me. When the sun rose, you rubbed your eyes, leaving specks of dried blood on your face. Then you went inside, got changed, and went to work. No one made breakfast for the kids, or lunch. They stayed in their closet-sized room, holding each other, so still it seemed like they'd put down roots. I reached out for them, but my touch was mould in the corners and mildew in the walls.

You made me a rotten thing. I couldn't hold my own children without poisoning their lungs.

Moving on. You didn't call anyone about what happened. You just drank and waited. It took so much longer than you expected for anyone to notice I was gone. Even then, it seemed like nobody cared. I didn't work and rarely went outside. Even before you killed me, I was a ghost woman. The only difference now is that I can walk through walls, not just fade into them.

I never had any friends, my dear. If I had, then maybe it wouldn't have come to this. Or maybe I still would've picked you and we'd have ended up in exactly the same place—the both of us rotting in different ways. Me, working my way up through the mud, fruiting bodies sprouting from the ruins of muscle and bone, delicate thread-like hyphae dragging my corpse home; you, sitting in silence, staring at a blank screen, waiting to die. Waiting for me.

There are no flowers on my grave, just mushrooms growing up from the wreckage of my skin. Tiny roots prod at my ribcage. My tongue has turned to liquid in the ruins of my mouth. And you know what? I'm okay with that. I'd rather be mycelium than wildflower. After all, you can't kill a fungus in any way that matters. The bit you can see and eat is so much smaller than the whole. Some mushrooms are still alive when you bite into them. They do not breathe, they do not think—they just give off spores and wait. Everything breaks down eventually. You will, too.

Oh dear, now I've shown my hand. Well, it's not as though it's a surprise. You've felt it, haven't you? The way the air has grown thicker, damper, heavier since the kids were taken away? I'm coming back, darling. Black mould is my hair. The warts building up on your skin are my eyes. The wet, hacking coughs that grow worse with every passing hour are my kisses. Transparent fibres wrap around you where you sit, coiling like cobweb, holding you nice and still for me. Just outside these darkened halls, a decaying corpse with fungus growing through its skull reaches jerkily for the doorknob.

One more choice to make: a quiet sleep out here in the cold earth, or you.

I chose you, of course. I always choose you.

NICOLA KAPRON has previously been published by Neo-opsis Science Fiction Magazine, Nocturnal Sirens Publishing, Rebel Mountain Press, Soteira Press, All Worlds Wayfarer, and Mannison Press. Nicola lives in Nanaimo, British Columbia, with a hoard of books—mostly fantasy and horror—and an extremely fluffy cat.

HARROW

A.J. Van Belle

I sit on the edge of a claw-foot tub, unclothed. I open the trapdoor in my leg and remove the expired power cell. My amplification systems require extra energy, and this cell is drained. I take a new one from a pile of replacements on a shelf and remove its vacuum wrap. The sterile gloves are necessary, but I do not like them. They reduce my sensitivity, and I use them only for this and for rare work with open wounds in others.

I am not primarily a surgeon. I'm a healer. There is a difference.

Rain whips the bathroom window. Thunder shakes the house's foundation.

The cell snaps into place, an alien thing that both is and is not part of me. The buzz of its energy makes my skin crawl, but as it works, my nerves calm. The hunger is still there, the sense I'm drawn out thin. But the excess drain is gone. The cell now powers my augmentations. I am warp and weft of flesh and silicon. An abomination in homeostasis.

I live in a valley rich with flowers and water and soil that runs with minerals that nourish my garden.

Another crash of thunder. This one rocks the floor and sends vibrations through my feet. The storm will pass quickly. Clouds blow in and out here as fast as my fleeting memories.

I am this planet's sole permanent inhabitant. We made sure of that before we built my house here. It's styled after something I never saw. An Earth country manor house, from the days before the Rising, the melting of the ice caps that raised the seas. But I'd read about country manors. They said I could have anything, and so I chose this.

I drop the cell's wrapper into the waste container, as an ordinary human might cast aside the wrapper for a razor or a tampon. Still naked, I comb out my wet hair. It has remained golden.

I've lost track of my years, but the modifications slow aging. My rough calculation puts me perhaps in my early seventies, but I've changed little since the operation series, and… I know when that was. Thirty-three years ago. I've lost most of the memory from before. I was neither young nor old at the time, perhaps in my forties.

I suppose I could trawl the Nebula and find the year of my birth. But that is of little interest to me.

I replace the comb on the shelf. My hair hangs heavy to my waist. I do remember that before the change, I couldn't grow hair past my upper back. It would go thin and scraggly at the ends, so I kept it trimmed to shoulder length. Was I a woman, then, since that's the fashion for women more than men? I suppose I was.

No one has hailed me with a request to land tonight, so I'll be alone all evening, as usual. I go downstairs naked.

What I label myself—man or woman, human or beast—is immaterial. I am what I do. I am a healer. But I heal by taking my patients through the darkest depths of their nightmares. Hence my name. Harrow.

The only way to end disease at its root is to dig deep into the soil. Turn the worms and other sightless creatures out of their loamy beds. Wrench metaphorical bullets from beneath long-healed flesh.

I enter the kitchen and pour myself a glass of juice from the fruit of the Cazry tree. I lean against the counter, enjoying the pulse of energy from the cell, recharging my auxiliary systems. Outside, the Cazry tree is in bloom. Big, white blossoms as large as my hand, fluttering in a storm wind. Some are scattered over the ground at the base of the tree.

A noise behind me, a clatter above the sighing of the wind. I turn.

Gray-blue light streams into the hall; the front door is open. Must have been the wind.

No. A shadow blocks the light in the hallway. So. A seeker, come without permission. “I’m unclad,” I call out. Dry, unamused.

I first see him not as a human but as a movement, a stagger, a fall. And there he is in the hall, in a pool of his own blood.

I set my glass on the table and move to his side. His eyelids flutter, a reflex that tells me there’s no point asking him why he came to me half dead or how he got to my planet. A glance through the open door reveals a steaming hunk of metal resting off kilter next to my vegetable garden, a long mud track showing the angle of its slide in. Scratches and dirt mar the space pod’s exterior. Second-hand and picked up on the black market, no doubt. And it is not supposed to be here.

I slide my arms under the man's shoulders and hips, lift him, and take him to the healing room. I lay him out on the table and rip his shirt open with my hands. Entrails glisten through the wound in his abdomen. Yellow fat cells gleam at the edges of the torn skin. I sterilise the area with a combination of light from ultra- and infra-spectrum lamps, the natural energy from my hands, and the frequencies from my implants. When the implants buzz to life, they raise disgust in me as always, these human inventions that don't belong beneath my skin.

He moans. Good. He's alive enough to feel pain.

My scan reveals the intestines are intact. Another good sign. There will be no sepsis. But he's lost almost three pints of blood and is losing more fast. I must work quickly. I secure the wound with sterile clamps, and then I stitch the edges. Fast, crudely, a sailmaker's whipstitch. The small needle punctures may scar. I do not have time to make this pretty.

When the stitches are in place, I angle my bioenergy at the region to warm the flesh, and then I beam electromagnetism from my implants. My eyes close as I work.

There is a trance-like quality to beaming, and in the brainspace it creates, memories often creep. *Fighter plane controls in my hands. Sweat dripping into my eyes. A canyon speeding below me.*

No. Not now. The memory fragment means nothing. I beat it back.

My patient moans again. His legs twitch.

I am a walking, breathing version of a healing-magnechamber. The implants are illegal. I was created in secret, and this is why I live in seclusion.

The edges of the wound close part-way, leaving a furious broken pink fault line across the landscape of his abdomen. I remove the clamps and let the skin subside into its natural position. I yank the suture thread out with one quick movement. It is like pulling a shoelace free from a shoe. Then I resume beaming. The skin closes the rest of the way.

A hand grabs my wrist. I give him a look that says, *Seriously?*

He lets go and raises his head from the table, half-lidded eyes, pale face, lips whitish and dry. "Are you who I think you are?"

I want to know who he thinks I am and how he stumbled onto my planet, but now is not the time to ask. I give him a cold smile. "Do you meet many seven-foot-tall nonbinary cyborg healers?"

He drops my wrist and his head falls back. "You're… naked."

"In my own home. *Alone* in my home, or so I thought."

"And all patchy," he adds, eyes closed. "Like an… overripe banana."

He has the colours wrong. I'm tan and cream, not bright yellow and dark brown.

"And you don't have boy parts or girl parts," he adds, sounding sleepy.

He needs blood. My internal sensors tell me he's O positive. I start an IV, and he naps through the needle's insertion. I give him a pint and a half of synthesised blood. His body can replenish the rest quickly enough. During the transfusion, I scan him more thoroughly, looking for invisible injuries. I'm unsurprised to detect a concussion. There's no danger of bleeding on the brain, so I will treat the injury later. I don't mind the chance to question him while his thought processes are compromised.

I stop with my palms a few centimetres above his forearm. Not everything beneath his skin is flesh and bone.

I scan the other arm. That one too has implants similar to mine. I scowl and clench my fists.

"How did you find me?" I whisper, soft, angry words. He doesn't stir. I stride to the sink in the corner, wet a washcloth, and sluice his blood from my torso.

He wakes up halfway through the transfusion, as I finish washing. He says nothing but watches me, more alert but quieter now. I drop the cloth in the sink and pull on a lab coat. I have mine specially made, of softer material than the usual. Comfort and freedom of movement are my main concerns, though the pearly off-white of the coat does put some patients at ease, those who expect a traditional doctor.

I sit on my tall stool near the table. "Now," I say. "How did you receive that wound?" There are other things I'm more curious about, but as a healer, I should always frame my first questions around the patient's needs.

"Miscalculated when I came in to land. Hit the ground too hard, got thrown around inside the pod. Think I hit an open cabinet door."

On high impact, that would slice through him indeed. I nod. "What's your name?"

"Davorin. From Aethra. No—that wasn't the latest place." He puts a hand to his forehead. "Let me think."

"It's fine. Who sent you here?"

His hand drops to his side again and his forehead wrinkles. "Only me. Months of searching. Rumours... heard there was someone who could... could help me." His eyes fall closed.

I glide away and return with a shirt of mine to lend him, a simple white tunic. "You need sleep. Come." I coax him to a sitting position and help him put on the shirt like a child. He's blurry around the edges, obedient. I take him to a spare bedroom on the second floor. My usual guests are soldiers, injured on missions the interstellar military hides even from its own. They often stay overnight. Davorin wavers in the bedroom doorway. "Why are you so tall? Were you that tall before?"

"I don't think so. And I don't know why." Somewhere outside the edges of memory, I think the military meant me for something else first, a plan that didn't work out. This hidden-away bio-radiant medic arrangement was not their first intention.

Davorin seems to sleep as soon as he is horizontal on the soft, white-sheeted bed. My sensors tell me his concussion remains stable, so I leave and climb the stairs to the observatory at the top level of the house to think.

Night has fallen, and the clouds are gone for now. The stars shine down through the glass-roofed observatory. No matter the reason Davorin sought me, now there's one person who knows how to find me, besides the small secret faction that made me. My existence is illegal. I have no fear of death, but I am useful. I help those others cannot. If I'm found by the lawmakers and destroyed, that will end.

I close my eyes and travel within myself, shutting out the sound of the wind howling around the corners of the house. This unauthorised seeker wants some sort of help. Whether I give it or not, he'll go away and put me and my work in danger. He knows the way here now. There's no undoing that. Not without destroying him.

The thought sends a jolt of pain through my body, like electricity, bringing me more to life but stinging every cell. *Murder.* Destroying him would be easy for me, physically. But could I live with knowing what I did?

It would be worth this one life, for the many I will save over the years. "It is a far better thing that I do…" From a very old fiction. Words spoken about self-sacrifice.

But I already sacrificed myself long ago. Life itself is not worth saving. Death is no tragedy. We all die. We all are energy. When we die, our energy stops being rounded up into masses of cells. We are but entropy-fighting machines, and we are wimps in the face of it. I have a few extra systems in place to fight it off longer than most. One day, perhaps a long time from now, or sooner if I choose, I will release my energy and let it swirl among the stars. And that will be neither a day for celebration nor lamentation. It will be a day like any other. The seed grows. The fruit falls. The fruit rots. I shall rot too, except for the implants, which one day too will melt when a supernova grows hot enough and engulfs this planet.

There is no god. There is no end. There is only cycling, a dance of energies, changing form, twining about one another, meeting and forming and separating and reforming.

We are all one.

Killing is not a sin. There is no such thing as sin. And, in a sense, there is no such thing as killing.

I hug my knees to my chest and grip my upper arms, eyes still closed, mind still within. My arms feel wrong under my own touch. I don't belong in this body or this life, but I know nothing else. The implants fire up and each hand beams electromagnetism into the opposite arm. *Flash and I'm outside, barefoot on the grass, smelling smoke from the crash-landed pod and loam from the churned-up ground. The pod hatch stands open. It's an old vessel, with the nitrogen-catalysed converter in the main chamber. A few crossed wires could—*

I draw in a sharp breath and open my eyes. I'm sitting in the observatory. My feet are damp and cool, with a film of dirt on the soles, but weren't they that way already?

The feel of wires in my hands. Hot with potential. I used to know every type of vessel for sky and space. So easy to—

I look up at the stars twinkling coldly through the glass roof. My breaths come fast, as if I've run up the stairs. But I haven't moved.

I slide off the seat and walk down the stairs with measured steps. My thoughts slow, like still water. I am a healer. I am a creator. I am one who does not kill.

Have I? Did I, before I allowed this transformation? I can't remember that either.

Halfway down the second flight of stairs, I sense a heart beating behind me and turn. Davorin stands like a shadow on the landing above, his face in darkness.

I wait a long moment for him to say something, but he does not, so I speak first. "Well, if you're coming downstairs, come on."

He follows. "I maybe slept a little. Mostly couldn't."

"You seemed to sleep. But you weren't in bed long."

He draws back a few centimetres. "Felt like hours." He follows me down the stairs. "I think it *was* hours. Still not thinking straight, though. I would ask if you can fix that too, but…" He trails off.

I lead the way to the kitchen. Cool shades of multi-moonlight stripe the floor. "But what?"

He stumbles, catches himself against the door frame. "I know what you were thinking. While you were wandering through the house. When you thought I was asleep." He says these sentences like a gamble. Like playing his hand when he's not sure it's good enough.

"Really."

"It's one of the changes they made. Could you detect it? The mind stuff, I mean."

"You're not seriously telling me you can read minds."

"No. No, not the way you would imagine. I read waveforms. The way you read my pulse and other vital signs? I read the electromagnetic signals of your mind. I can translate what I sense into general emotions and intentions. Nothing too specific." He balls up a fist and holds it in the air a long moment before tapping it against the wall. A controlled, quiet slam. "I'm like you. I'm not a regular person anymore. I'm... constructed. I don't want it. You're like me. You're a doctor. A surgeon. I want it gone."

"I'm not a surgeon. I'm a healer," I correct.

"Whatever. Put me back the way I was."

"You've been enhanced. Like me. And you want me… to undo it," I muse aloud. "I could remove the implants in your arms, but I can't undo what they did to your mind. I wouldn't know where to start. Depending how they did it, trying to reverse it could cause you a lot of damage."

Davorin rests his head in his hand, elbow on the kitchen table. My glass of juice rests precariously close to that elbow. There are already enough blood-red messes to clean up around the house today. I move the glass.

"I was promised a shiny happily ever after," he mumbles, and I wonder if I've heard him correctly. "I was supposed to become the finest doctor in the richest city. As long as I passed them information, I would have my pick. Tesso. New Dubai. Denver. One of the big ones. But something went wrong. They wouldn't tell me what. I was discharged from the military. They said my alterations were invisible, so I could live a normal life."

I snort.

He continues as if he hasn't heard my derision. "I was trained in medicine, so I looked for a job. But I couldn't be around people. Feeling what they think… it's no good. Too much."

I extend my senses to his neurons. Past the slow pulse of injury, there is something different. So subtle I wouldn't have detected it without being told. "I think reversing that would kill you."

He doesn't answer, but his expression is fragile. He has not let go of hope.

"Come with me." I lead him to the observatory on the top floor of my home. Some decisions are best made under the stars. We could go outside, yes. But the observatory will make us feel somehow closer to the suns of other star systems. The grass is too close to the soil, too removed from the lofty skies, to let us remember the truth of our smallness in the universe. In contrast, the cold steel and vinyl of the observatory reminds us we're only elements ourselves.

He sits on the steel bench by the window that overlooks the garden. Looks out through the window and ignores the sky above. Figures.

I sit on the other end of the bench, careful not to touch him. Touch would ruin this. It would make me seem too human. I must be a machine in his eyes, if I am to have the desired effect. "You are willing to risk your life. But I'm not."

And there. It's out. My truth. I can't kill.

I *should* be a machine. Not just act like one. But there's nothing to be done about the weakness of emotions, of attachment. I am not the enlightened machine atop the pillar of existence. I am… I was… a human being. I have distaste for harming my almost-fellow humans. Inclinations to see them safe.

Inclinations based on illusions. I prolong my patients' lives, but I am not sprouting futures out of my capable hands. Only more dry branches. On and on we go like this. Spinning useless webs.

He looks at me askance and hugs a knee to his chest. "I just want to be normal again." He gets up. Walks away to the window on the far side of the room.

The moon trio has risen. Each moon has its own cool shade. Thalassa's is sapphire. Pan's is purple. And Nomus is a deep royal blue. The moons do not have official names. This planet is uninhabited; why should its moons have names? Because *I* live here, that's why. And so I named them.

Davorin stands bathed in the blue-purple light. He's a ghost except for one fist clenching at his side. "I want to go back. To the way it was before. I want to be the person I was before I knew all… this." He sweeps the other hand up and down himself. "The implants. The brain. The... *knowing*. Everything. I want to be an ordinary human. Not a freak."

"If you're a freak," I say, "I *sure* as hell am one."

He jumps. "I didn't mean—"

"Don't pretend you think I'm offended."

He puts a fist and forearm high on the glass and leans forward. Rests his forehead against the arm and gazes out at the moons half-rimmed above the trees. "I've been practicing. Turning it backward."

Now he makes no sense. "You can't undo it. From what I sense, your neurons are re-tuned. Even if the same surgeons reversed the implants and changes, you'd be altered. You'd—"

“That’s not what I mean.” His voice is quiet, almost lyrical. But it cuts through my own words like a scalpel through soft flesh. “I’ve been turning the med beams… inside out. Have you done it?”

Done what? I don’t say the words out loud, just let him read my questioning vibe in the air.

“You want me to spell it out,” he says. “Fine. Have you harmed instead of helped? Have you made it into an un-med beam? One that hurts?”

“That’s not possible.”

He turns away from the window and hovers a palm over his other forearm. His forehead scrunches. I wait long seconds. A dark weal spreads over the forearm. He closes the distance between us in one stride, bends forward, and places the wounded arm inches from my face. “Tell me again it’s not possible.”

Coldness creeps through my arms and fingers. “How far have you taken it?”

“Insects,” he says, standing straighter and pulling his arm away. He cradles it close to his side. I feel the pain coming from him in waves. “Mice. It’s easy. The only thing I don’t know is whether I could take it far enough on myself. Can I stay conscious long enough to pass the point of no return? I don’t know. And I get one shot. If I do it, but don’t finish the job… who knows what I’ll be when I’m done. Half-alive roadkill.” He turns a hollow gaze to me. “But I don’t want to live anymore. Unless you can make me normal again.”

“I can’t,” I say. “There is no normal.”

"Try?" The word comes out as a soft plea. "I can't think. Head hurts."

I rise and gesture for him to follow me. He does, without a word. Down the two long flights of narrow stairs. Back to the first floor. Back to the healing room.

What am I doing? Minutes ago, I considered giving him a quick end in his sleep. Now I plan to heal his bruised brain so he can decide whether to live or die. I am a military secret, known only to the small sub-branch that created me illegally so they can keep me hidden on this "uninhabited" planet to heal the victims of illicit special ops. I was not made to heal wounded sparrows. Or to give them choices.

I tell him to take his place on the table. To ensure the beams from my hands and implants will reach his brain, I use a cap that amplifies the signal, an electrified half-shell of silver and graphite.

"Close your eyes," I tell him, but they're already closed. I close my own, and a flash of memory sweeps me like a wave.

I remember being something different. Not this robed figure in a house built of imagined nostalgia. Something more human, but not as safe.

Sweat from my palms dripped down the control grips. The prone flying position was my favourite, the best for tight manoeuvres, but it increased my body's adrenaline response. Could be dangerous, if my heart rate went too high, my breathing too rapid, and my mental acuity decreased from stress. But usually, it struck the perfect balance for me, kept me right on the edge, where I was sharpest.

The unnamed planet's harsh landscape sped by below me, and as my plane zigged its way through a chasm, I made decisions in microseconds to avoid sharp outcroppings. This was not the way to live a long life, but it was the way for me to be alive.

"Almost there, H3," said the nav officer. The crackling of the speaker told me the chasm walls were interrupting the signal. But I needed to know what he had to say. Balance between flying too high and being seen and shot down... and going too low and losing the signal.

I shake off the past. I still don't want it.

My sensors tell me Davorin's bruising is going down. My hands are as hot as a tea kettle. With my energy entwined with his, and now that I know what to look for, I feel the change more clearly. The sensitivity of his brain cells turned up. If they were wires, his neurons would be higher voltage than the ordinary human's. I don't know how it was done. I have no means of reversing it.

I bow my head and focus on healing.

The flashes come only when I work. Flashes of the truth, the path that stretches behind me, all rubble and ruin…

...and times I had to look up into the eyes of another human being, because I was tall, but not this tall. I remember shaving, shaving something, not sure what body part but I recall the feel of the razor and the tiny snick of each hair chopped off at the skin and I see the light of a red-orange sun that made everything right once but not now and blood runs into a drain and I'm crying...

…and this was long ago, before the change, some part of the normal ups and downs of life I can't recall.

I shift my hands, reach deeper into his being with the radiant vibration of my implants. Tell myself to stay in the moment. Stay. Here. Now.

But another one hits me—this one familiar, from the change I'm sure, though it floats without context, without bearing or ballast: *the green light, the hands. The sound of screaming pelting every inch of my flesh, and I don't know why my throat is raw.*

There's no pain in the memory. There must have been, searing my mind, or I would not recall the rest. But I can't remember the pain.

The real memory, the sort I can pull out and examine, begins in a room without the green light. With a soft white blanket. With clean sheets. With newborn cyborg limbs.

I remember the door opening and someone coming in with a tray of food. I sat up. I reached toward the person in the pale-blue scrubs. And I said a name. I don't know what name. It's the only thing I can't remember about that scene.

I remember all too clearly how the aide's expression fell shut like a door slamming, how they left as if the name were poison.

Did a loved one die? Did I ask for someone who was gone?

Was I gone, already, then?

As my healing beams reach the darkest part of his mind, he arches his back. Veins pop out on his arms, forehead, neck. His scream pulses through the walls of my house and through the soft gel of my marrow. With my mind's eye, I see his skeleton through the skin, alight with the pain every human keeps buried. To the echo of the scream, he falls back, muscles slack.

When it's done, I lift the radiant cap, and Davorin opens his eyes. He flexes his left hand, lifts it to the light. It looks… like a hand. But I imagine the light passing through it, illuminating veins, making the fragile netting of skin glow red.

Energy still flows through me, skimming memories I've locked away. There are bits, moments. *Riding in a vehicle, laughing, another knee sticky with sweat against mine because there were too many of us for the seat but we liked it that way.*

But who is *we* and was I ever really someone like that, a person who made up one cog in the giant machine of humanity, frail and faulty on my own but strong in companionship? It is like a window into another life now. Perhaps it is. Perhaps it was. Another life, that is.

"Could you feel what they did to my mind?" he asks in a hoarse voice. "Can you undo it?"

"I did feel it," I tell him. "But I told you I sensed it already. And I told you I can't undo it."

My head jerks back. I have a view of the ceiling before I understand: Davorin has wrapped his hand in my long hair and pulled. He sits up and snarls, low. "You can't keep it all for yourself."

"Keep what?" My voice is strained through my hyper-extended throat. I choose not to fight him. Not yet. I want him to think he has the upper hand.

"This fucking planet. Your solitude. The whole… being okay with being… what we are."

He pulls harder on my hair, then lets it go. I bring my head back to its upright position and look over him at the far wall. "What I do has no effect on you. There's enough solitude in the universe to go around." Many times over. "And you're in control of whether you accept what you are." Is he? Are we?

He leaps to his feet, hands in fists, the red welt standing out on his forearm even in the dimness. "It's *not* what I am. I'm trapped in this body. And it's not me."

I should say nothing, but I am not good at doing what I should do when it comes to human interactions. "I hate to break it to you, but it *is* you. It may not be what you used to be, but it's what you are now."

"If you don't help me," he says in a low voice, "I'll tell them where to find you. You'll be killed."

Flash and I see myself in his eyes. I see me for the first time in decades. I see now I have been correct. I am not human. I am remade, something new, a cryptid demigod. *Wires in my hands. So easy to reconfigure them, to reverse the ship's fight against entropy, explode it into the void.* Is that a memory or a fantasy?

I don't want to see myself. I don't want to see how much I lack. I want to know what it is to breathe and to move crosswise through space, slicing across waves of the space-time continuum instead of only riding the waves of time here in one place. But I do not want to want this. I have walled it off. This man embodies the desires I keep locked away. My desire to destroy him—it is only the desire to destroy myself, a childlike confusion that leads me to stomp on a broken toy.

"Come outside," I order. Now we need the smallness. Closeness to the soil. We need to know we're only earthworms, crawling things, ineffectual.

His eyes are focused now. Hard, suspicious, and clear on what he wants. Whether that's to die, or to take revenge on me for refusing to try to change him back, I can't be sure. We go out the front door. Cloud cover has returned, blotting out stars and moons and threatening more rain. The wind whips my hair to mermaid wildness. I stand barefoot in the grass and face him as water drips from the twigs of a Cazry tree and strikes my face and neck.

"You're going to go away from here," I tell him. "I'm not afraid of your threat. You won't tell anyone you found me here, because you won't want to. My existence will go on as it was. I'm going to show you why." Under the Cazry trees, I sit cross-legged on the grass. He sits across from me, as if compelled. I don't touch him. This is one of those moments when you could imagine the hermit healer takes the hands of the seeker and shows him the ephemeral zephyrs of the mind that whisper around mountain crags. But my mountain is a planet and my mind is more than a zephyr. I do nothing but pick up a fallen fruit and break it in half between my palms. Red juice runs over my hands like blood. He looks at me as if wondering if he should do the same, if this is some required ritual action. But he only twirls a blade of grass between his thumb and forefinger. "It doesn't matter if the fruit is broken or not," I say. "It already fell from the tree." I don't have words to explain further, so I wait and see if he picks up the brainwaves and understands.

He curls his lip in scorn. "You're not a fruit. You're a human being."

"Not anymore. You can't break me in any way that matters to me. There's nothing I'm afraid of." *Except one. The thing you ask of me.*

A streak of lightning rips the distant sky, turning everything green for a moment. Davorin makes a noise of exasperation and stands up. "Thanks for keeping me from dying." His tone says *thanks for nothing.*

He walks away from me as the first raindrops splatter us. He is leaving. Now. Taking one of my shirts.

Where rain hits his back, the white of the shirt turns grey, clinging to his skin. Thunder rolls, the sound of the sky cracking.

I return to my doorway. Behind me, the pod hums to life as drops fall faster, and the engine sound merges with the rain splatter. The faint smell of exhaust mingles with the storm's ozone scent.

Another crack. The thunder is nothing new.

But the smell of electrical fire makes me turn. The pod grows small, a shadow lost against the dark sky. Another crack sounds, this one louder, and it is not thunder. No more than the crash landing that shook my feet hours ago.

A line of light appears along the edge of the pod's now-tiny, distant shape. The line rotates. The hull cracks. Brilliance hatches from a metal egg.

Then in a shower of sparks, like fireworks I remember (*from where?*) the pod explodes. It is brilliant, blue, green, and white, lighting up a towering city of clouds. Rain extinguishes the sparks before they reach the treetops.

The pod must have been fatally damaged when it hit the ground.

Or Davorin sabotaged it himself. Because, if I couldn't help him, he wanted to die.

The hatch opens at my touch. Wires in my hands.

I never touched the pod. I chose to let him go free.

I heal by taking patients through the depths of their nightmares.

The light in the sky burns itself out. Nothing but ash reaches the ground.

I hold out a hand, flesh and silicon. A curl of charred metal floats to land in the well of my palm. It is as frail as a dry leaf.

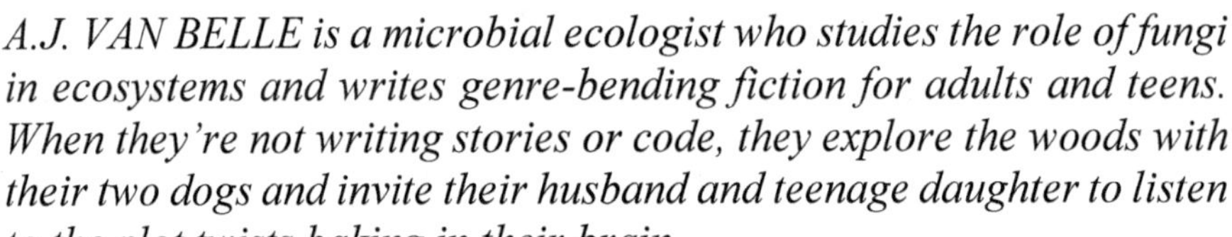

A.J. VAN BELLE is a microbial ecologist who studies the role of fungi in ecosystems and writes genre-bending fiction for adults and teens. When they're not writing stories or code, they explore the woods with their two dogs and invite their husband and teenage daughter to listen to the plot twists baking in their brain.

CONTENT WARNINGS

SIPHONOPHORE by Saoirse Ní Chiaragáin

Rape / assault, sexual coercion, mutilation.

THICKER THAN WATER by Kristin Cleaveland

Bereavement, pregnancy loss, postpartum depression, inherited mental illness.

GASTRIC by Caitlin Marceau

Fatphobia, disordered eating, emetophobia, weight-loss surgery.

MILK by Sally Hughes

Post-natal depression / psychosis.

IT WON'T BE SO BAD by Varian Ross

Pregnancy, body horror, unreality (an AI meant to simulate birth,) death, and gaslighting.

WHAT GOES DOWN, MUST COME UP by Evelyn Freeling

Eating disorders, bulimia, anorexia, emetophobia.

FIRST HARVEST by April Yates

Reference to infertility.

TOO HEAVY TO CARRY by Faye Snowden

Slavery, physical violence, abuse of slaves, child abuse.

FACES OF SETH by Vivian Kasley

Rape, sexual coercion, child sexual abuse, trauma flashbacks.

BLOOM by Alice Austin

None.

BLESSED ART THOU AMONG WOMEN by Vashelle Nino

Religious references, body image issues.

THE GLOBE by Cecilia Kennedy

Fatphobia, weight-loss surgery, self-injury.

HYSTERICAL by Lindsay King-Miller

Pregnancy loss, self-injury, infertility.

KNIT, PURL by Nicole M. Wolverton

Self-injury.

JULIE by Victoria Nations

Binge eating, body image issues.

CLIPPED WINGS by Emma Kathryn

Domestic abuse, self-injury.

SKIN DEEP by Petina Strohmer

Coercion, plastic surgery, self-image issues.

DODO TI PITIT MANMAN by Michelle Mellon

Reference to infertility.

WRITTEN ON HER SKIN by Nico Bell

Verbal abuse, threat, implied self-injury.

A ROTTEN THING by Nicola Kapron

Domestic abuse / violence.

HARROW by A.J. Van Belle

Dissociation, body dysphoria, implied suicidal thoughts.

ACKNOWLEDGEMENTS

From the first conception of this anthology idea, I've been overwhelmed by the support and positivity of the writing / horror community. Your enthusiasm and willingness to support new publishers is heartening and wonderful to see.

Thanks to everyone who sent stories (I wish I could have taken more), shared our updates on social media, bought books, joined our Patreon, and offered sympathy and support on difficult days. Special thanks to Alex for the fantastic foreword, and to all our contributors who were willing to dig deep and come up with these superb, powerful stories. It's such an honour to be trusted with your work.

Much love,

Antonia

ALSO AVAILABLE FROM GHOST ORCHID PRESS

Dark Hearts: Tales of Twisted Love

ghostorchidpress.com

www.ingramcontent.com/pod-product-compliance
Lightning Source LLC
LaVergne TN
LVHW010053170826
845678LV00012B/2130

* 9 7 8 1 8 3 8 3 9 1 5 8 4 *